Mother Awe

and other stories

THE BAILEY

CAPTAIN CHRISTMAS

THE GREEN MAN

THE DARKEATER

WINSTON PARNELL &

THE PRIESTESS OF MARS

David Spangler

Mother Awe and Other Stories
By David Spangler

Edited by Julia Spangler

Illustrations:

MOTHER AWE - Deva Berg
THE BAILEY - Kaitlin Spangler
CAPTAIN CHRISTMAS - Kaitlin Spangler
THE GREEN MAN - Jeremy Berg
THE DARKEATER - Deva Berg
WINSTON PARNELL & THE PRIESTESS OF MARS

ISBN 13: 978-1-939790-61-3

Spangler, David
Mother Awe and Other Stories / David Spangler

First Edition: February 2023

LorianPress LLC
Douglas, Michigan

www.lorian.org

Dedication

I dedicate these stories to you, dear Reader, in the hope they will bring you pleasure, delight, and even thoughtful moments.

Contents

Acknowledgements

I want to acknowledge my lovely and talented wife, Julia, who edited all these stories and serves as an inspiration for my storytelling every year. I also want to acknowledge my daughter Kaitlin, her husband Josh, and my dear friends and colleagues, Jeremy Berg and his daughter, Deva. They are responsible for all the lovely illustrations in this book. Jeremy also sees that they get published, which is a true gift. Thank you, my friend! And acknowledgments as well for all the friends and family who every year encourage me to write another story and support me in meeting the challenge of doing so. I love you all!

And to the Inner Muse from whom all stories come, thank you!

FOREWORD

This is my fourth anthology of stories. They are written to send to family and friends at Christmas time, so they share themes appropriate to the Holiday. However, they are stories celebrating the wonder that exists in the world around us every day of the year, so I like to think they are not simply Christmas stories. Mostly, they are meant to entertain and bring joy. If they also inspire a moment of thoughtfulness about the magic of life, then they have more than fulfilled their intent.

A word about the last story in this anthology, "Winston Parnell and the Priestess of Mars." Over a decade ago, over the course of three years, I wrote three short stories for Christmas paying homage to some of my favorite authors. One of these was "Dragon's Ride," a tribute to J. R. R. Tolkien; it has already been published by Lorian Press in the anthology, *Starheart and Other Stories*. A second was my attempt to write a Stephen King-like ghost story. It was OK, but I always felt it needed some more work before being more widely published. I imagine it will eventually show up in one of these anthologies.

The third, though, was a tribute to two of my favorite fictional characters: Sherlock Holmes and John Carter of Mars, and I had a lot of fun writing it. Their respective authors, Sir Arthur Conan Doyle and Edgar Rice Burroughs (famous as the creator of Tarzan of the Apes) have given me many hours of enjoyment over the years. In their different ways, they both wrote ripping good yarns! I wanted to capture the gaslight feel of a Victorian world where Britain ruled most of the world, people believed in mysteries, spiritualism, and the occult, and Mars was thought to possess vast canals and ruined cities. It was an era the pulp novels gleefully explored.

When I wrote this story, my literary agent at the time liked it and encouraged me to expand it into a full novel. I was certainly willing, but I never quite found the time nor to be honest, the full inspiration I needed to do so. So, this story has been languishing in my files for several years. I felt it was past time for it to see print.

I hope all these stories delight you in their own way and bring you as much pleasure in the reading as I have had in the writing.

MOTHER AWE

For the first thirteen years of my life, my mother disappeared the day before Christmas. On the day after Christmas, I would wake up and she would be home again, humming or singing in the kitchen as she made breakfast for Dad and me. But for two days—for me, the most important days of the year except for my birthday—she would be gone.

I never knew where she went. When I asked Dad, he would smile and say, "Your Mom had to work." When I asked her, she would say, "I'm sorry I wasn't here, but I had things I had to do." In all those years, though, neither of them ever said just what her work was or what those "things" she had to do were. If I pressed too much, they both would come up with the ultimate conversation-ender for a child: "You'll know when you're old enough."

When I was a young child, I took this pattern as normal. After all, what else did I know? It was Christmastime, so Mom would be away for a couple of days. Dad was always there, and he made sure we had a great day together. We would open presents and then do something special. Then, when Mom came back the next day, we would open more presents with her. It was like having two Christmases instead of one. It was after I started school and began comparing notes with my friends, whose mothers did not vanish over Christmas, that I began to wonder and ask questions. Questions that were never answered.

Until I was thirteen.

Aside from this peculiarity, I had an ordinary childhood. Actually, it was more than ordinary. My Mom more than made up for not being with me on Christmas Day. For her, everyday was special, and she made it so for me, too.

The house I grew up in was a sprawling one-story adobe house with a three-story, flat-roofed tower at one end. That is where my father had his mini-observatory, which basically consisted of a computerized Celestron telescope, a chair, and a table for his laptop. He worked as a cosmologist and astronomer at the Kitt Observatory, south of Tuscon, Arizona. You may have heard of him. He was the "astronomer poet" who was often a guest on Neil deGrasse Tyson's television show, *Star Talk*. Our home was located far enough from the city that our view of the sky was relatively unpolluted by the lights of Tuscon at night.

My Dad is a sensitive, kind, witty man who went into astronomy because he fell in love with the cosmos. Most people don't take him for a scientist when they first meet him. They think he's an artist of some kind, and as I said, he *is* a poet. His poems about the beauty of the universe have been published in two best-selling books. My mother says she fell in love with him because he could hear the stars sing both in sky and in her. But he's also one of the top cosmologists and mathematicians in his field.

One of my mother's favorite things to do with me was to take a blanket and pillows up onto the flat roof of the tower late at night and lie there with me, looking up at the star-filled night sky. When my Dad had me look through the telescope, he would say, "There's Vega," "There's Andromeda," or "That whirlpool galaxy is Messier 81." He talked like an astronomer.

Not so my mother. When she pointed out stars to me, it was as if she was pointing out friends we saw in our neighborhood. "That's the Dancing Child," she would say, or "That star is the Hooded Lady. She's shy but she's having a secret affair with that bright one over there, the Man with the Shining Forehead."

The fact is, everything in the world was alive for my mother. She didn't name everything, but she still thought of everything as a person, whether it was the toaster that popped up my hot English muffins to me in the morning or the lizards that scampered along our back wall.

As a child, I found this enchanting. It was as if my mother was part of a whole other world and delighted in introducing me to her friends. As I got older and was more interested in fitting into the world of my classmates, I found her at times embarrassing.

Especially when I might have two of my "worldlier" friends over from school, and they found my mother carrying on a conversation with our couch. She laughed it off as just a fun way to do the housekeeping, but I worried for days after that the word would spread around the school that I had a crazy mother and therefore might be crazy myself.

It didn't. As it turned out, most of my friends' parents were bickering or splitting up. Strange as my mom might seem, my friends still sought her out for the loving, stress-free atmosphere she created around all of us.

Yet in the midst of an extraordinarily nice childhood, there was still this anomaly. Mom would disappear over Christmas.

Once, having heard a couple of my classmates discussing the "affairs" that had led to their parents divorcing, I wondered if Mom might have a secret lover. I found this thought both romantic and exciting on the one hand and threatening on the other. If this were true, I thought, it could lead to *my* parents splitting up. I desperately didn't want that to happen.

I confronted Dad about it one Christmas day when I was eleven.

"Dad, is Mom off with a lover? Is she having a "Same time next year" thing going on?" I'd seen the old Ellen Burstyn and Alan Alda movie on television the week before.

I think I was so blunt because I wanted to shock him. Asking nicely all those years hadn't gotten me any information about Mom's mysterious disappearances. I thought maybe confronting him with the idea of marital infidelity might knock some information loose. But he just laughed. "The whole world is your Mom's lover," he said. Then he mock frowned at me. "And what do *you* know about 'Same Time Next Year?'"

Dad insisted over the years that she was off doing her work, but Mom didn't have a job. She was a stay-at-home mother. What work would take her away from her family on Christmas Eve and Christmas Day? As I grew older, it made no sense. Further, there was never any sign of luggage or packing for a trip in the days leading up to Christmas, nor did I ever see her unpacking in the days after. It was as if she left with the clothes on her back and came back the same way.

Then there was the locked door.

My parents were pretty "free-range" when it came to giving me freedom. Not that there weren't appropriate boundaries, but they were flexible, and expanded as I got older and more responsible. However, one thing was always non-negotiable. The room on the other side of that locked door was forbidden territory.

The room itself was on the third floor of our Tower, part of a larger room that took up most of that floor. Its ceiling was the roof on which Mom and I would lie and tell stories about her friends in the stars. It could not be a large room, more, I guessed, like a walk-in closet that took up about a fourth of the third floor. When I asked one day what was in it, Mom said it was filled with special art supplies. This made sense. If the roof was ostensibly Dad's observatory, the third floor was my mother's craft space. It was essentially one large room, filled with tables and cabinets that held various art materials, fabrics, crystals, glass beads, feathers, and the like. Here my mother would make a variety of things that she would occasionally sell but mostly give away as gifts.

Given the plethora of things that were in the room, though, I couldn't imagine what else could be in the forbidden room. Naturally, I pleaded to be shown the "special art supplies," and always, maddingly, I was told no. Once when I tearfully and angrily asked why, Mom took me on her lap and said, "Sometimes a person has a special space that is only for them. Don't you have a place like that, one that's just for you, not for Dad or me, not for any of your friends?" I didn't, actually, but I understood what she meant.

After that, I resolved to get myself my own forbidden place just so I could tell Mom and Dad to keep out. And I did. It was a small two-drawer cabinet I kept in my closet. Funny thing is, I never actually bothered to put anything in to it. I've never been much for secrets, which is one reason Mom's locked room kept niggling at me. Or maybe I've not been into secrets because I hated that Mom was keeping one from me. Well, two, actually, counting her Christmas Day disappearances.

When I was twelve, my mother's sister Megan came to live with us. Aunt Megan was sweet and nice enough, but she was nothing like my mother. Mom was fair-haired while Megan was a dark brunette. Likewise, Mom was fair-skinned and Nordic in appearance, but Aunt Megan was darker, as if she had Italian or even Arabic ancestry. Further, Mom was an extrovert, always engaging with and enjoying people and life around her. Megan, on the other hand, was shy and seemed bemused by the world in which she found herself. It was hard to believe they were from the same family.

That is, until you saw their eyes. They had the same eyes, a pale blue that could go from soft to steel in an instant. My mother had a power in her eyes, one I never fully understood as a child. There was love in her gaze, certainly, but there was something else as well, as if her eyes had looked upon things beyond the ken of most humanity. Aunt Megan had the same eyes, filled with the same power.

Seeing their eyes, I knew without question they were sisters, however improbable that seemed just looking at their appearance.

For all her difference, Aunt Megan fit into our household like a hand into a glove. Dad told me it was the first he had met her, though he had heard Mom speak of her. He said she had lived in Europe but her husband had just died. Mom had invited her to come stay with us for a while, and she had accepted. Dad, being Dad, was gracious and welcoming and seemed to genuinely like her. I thought her strange, but being on the brink of teenage hood, I was feeling pretty strange myself.

Mom would spend part of her day tending her garden or doing things outside, where, in spite of her fair skin and Arizona's hot sun, she never seemed to tan, much less sunburn. Aunt Megan preferred to stay indoors. She spent hours in Mom's art room on the third floor of the Tower. While Mom liked to experiment and make large things, Megan made the most exquisite small pieces of jewelry, such as earrings and pins. In fact, she gained something of a local reputation as an artist when she took her creations to a local art fair and sold them all within a matter of a couple of hours.

Seeing an opportunity, I went into the art room one day when Megan was there alone. I watched as her fingers moved deliberately, shaping tiny pieces of metal and colored stones into the form of a vaguely beetle-like insect. I realized that she was manipulating these small items without the need for any kind of jeweler's magnification lens or even ordinary glasses. Even with my young eyes, I couldn't see the tiny pieces she was working with clearly enough to do what she was doing.

I watched in fascination for a time, then I remembered why I was there.

"Aunt Megan," I said, "Have you used any of the special art materials from Mom's closet there? The one that's locked?"

"Special art materials?" she asked, not looking up from what she was doing. I was hoping to pique her interest enough that she would gain access to the forbidden room, which, in turn, might give me a glimpse inside.

"Oh yes," I said. "For special projects. Maybe like what you're doing with your jewelry there." I pointed at the beetle-thing on the worktable.

She looked up at me, her eyes sparkling with humor. "You're trying to find out what's inside there, aren't you?"

Surprised at being so easily caught out, I stammered, "Oh.. oh, no. Not at all. I just thought you might like to use what's in there." I thought I'd recovered well.

"Maybe I would," she said. "What *is* in there?"

"Well…um…special art materials."

"Yes, that's what you said. Can you describe these materials for me?"

"Oh, I think it would be better if you saw them yourself. Then you would know if they were suitable. I doubt I could do them justice."

She laughed. It actually was the first time I'd heard her do so, and it was a lovely sound. Then she said the dreaded words. "If your mother hasn't shown you what's in there, then you'll find out when you're old enough." She turned her attention back to her piece of jewelry, the subject obviously closed.

How I hated those words: "When you're old enough." I was twelve, on the cusp of becoming a teenager. How old did I need to be?

That Christmas proved to be a turning point. I awoke on Christmas Eve Day to find Mom gone as she always was, but this time, Aunt Megan was gone with her.

This was too much! I'd been able to handle it when it was just Mom and Dad who knew where Mom went. It was strange, but I'd grown up with it. It was part of my normal life, even though as I'd gotten older, I'd felt more and more bugged by it. I always assumed I would discover what was going on, that I would be let into the mystery when the time was right—when I "was old enough." But now someone else had found out before me, assuming that Aunt Megan wasn't already part of the mystery. This was intolerable.

Ire rising, I stomped out of my bedroom as only a mad twelve-year old can and confronted my Dad who was making pancakes in the kitchen. I stood before him and said as fiercely as I could, "All right, Dad, tell me what's going on. Mom's gone as always, but now Aunt Megan's with her. Where are they? What's happening? And don't you dare tell me I'll find out when I'm old enough. I'm old enough now!"

I'm sure I was a ridiculous figure, standing there, arms akimbo in my Tiny Kitten pajamas, hair disheveled, bunny slippers on my feet. To his credit, he didn't laugh, though I'm sure he wanted to. I would have. Instead, he turned off the stove, set the pan with the half-cooked pancakes aside, and said, "Let's go into the living room and talk."

We went into the living room. In the corner, the Christmas tree lights were on and blinking their various colors. They would stay on all through the day and into the night until Mom returned. That was our tradition.

The morning sun was streaming into the picture window, but the room still felt chilly. Dad pulled out a blanket and spread it over us as we sat across from each other on the sofa. "Do you remember, Holly, how your mom and I met?"

This wasn't what I was expecting him to ask me, but I was quieting down. At least now, for the first time, I could tell I was going to get some information.

"You said you met her when she came to tour the observatory. You said the moment you saw her, you knew you were going to marry her and she felt the same with you. Love at first sight. Right?"

"Right. But it's not the whole story."

"Then what *is* the whole story? What haven't you two been telling me?" My usually witty father was looking so serious that I was beginning to feel anxious.

"Hold your horses, Miss Ants-In-Pants. I'm getting there. And it's nothing bad," he added, as if sensing my anxiety. "Only strange."

"Oh, OK. Strange I can deal with," I said, hoping it was true. How strange was "strange?"

"After I saw your mother in the tour group, I tried to find out who she was, but no one seemed to know. It seems she wasn't really part of the tour group. That is, she hadn't been on the tour bus that came up from Tuscon, or at least no one had noticed her."

"And that *would* be strange," I said. Mom was not someone no one would notice.

"I agree. And I thought so at the time. But if she hadn't come up with the tour, how had she come to be there? She could have driven up on her own, of course, but for some reason, I didn't think that she had. In any event, I had no trail to follow. She had been there and then she had disappeared."

"Must have been Christmas Eve day," I snorted.

Dad laughed. "No. It was the middle of the summer. Anyway, I didn't know what to do, so I had to put her out of my mind. But I couldn't! I found myself thinking about her all the time. I couldn't help myself. I'd really fallen for her."

I reached over and patted his arm. "Poor Dad," I said.

"Yeah, poor me. My boss didn't know what was wrong but he could see I was distracted. He told me to take a couple of days off and clear my head, as he put it. I agreed. I certainly wasn't getting my work done!"

He paused, remembering, then he went on. "I decided to go camping out in the desert, away from everything. Just lie under the night sky, watch the stars, maybe compose some verses. Yes, I was already writing poetry then. So that's what I did." He shifted under the blanket, stretching out his legs. When he got comfortable again, he continued. "My second night, I was sitting by my campfire, when I heard a noise. I thought it might be a coyote or something but then, your mother wandered into my camp."

"Mom? Out in the desert? She just wandered in?"

"She just wandered in. I was just as surprised as you are now. More! But...I don't know how to explain this, Holly. It seemed right. It seemed more than right. It was as if I'd been expecting her but hadn't known it. And now, here she was, standing by my campfire, smiling down on me."

"What was she wearing?"

"Wearing? What, you want a fashion rundown? She...she was wearing jeans and a flannel shirt and a white jacket of some kind. And boots. She had on boots. What?" he asked. I must have been looking disappointed.

"Oh, nothing. I don't know. I thought she might be wearing robes or something."

"Robes? On the desert?" he laughed. "No, no robes. Like I said, everything was ordinary, her clothes, the campfire…yet, it wasn't. It was extraordinary. How had she come to be there? How had she come to find me, in the middle of the night? Even I wasn't sure just where I was."

"Yes, yes!" Now I was excited. I felt on the edge of solving the mystery. It was as if the locked door to the forbidden room in the Tower was starting to open. "How had Mom come to be there?"

"I had her sit down next to me, and I asked her. And you know what she said?"

Suddenly, I knew—I don't know how—exactly what she'd said. "She said, 'I heard you singing to the stars and the stars in me answered.'"

Dad looked at me dumbfounded, as if the sofa had suddenly spoken to him instead of his daughter. "How…how did you know that?" Then, he relaxed and chuckled. "Of course! Mom must have told you. But did she tell you this story already?"

"No, she hasn't. And she didn't tell me those words, not exactly. But she did say she fell in love with you because you sing to the stars in the sky and in her."

He smiled. "She said that? That's nice. And yes, that's basically what she said that night. Of course, it answered nothing. It didn't tell me how she got there, without a car, or really how she found me. But you know what, Holly? I didn't care. The next morning, she got in my car with me and we drove back to Tucson and got married. Nine months later, you showed up."

"Me? You mean, that night, you did..It?" I grinned.

"You bet. You want the details?"

"Ew! No! But didn't you wonder? I mean…."

"I know what you mean. And yes, I did wonder. It didn't matter, Holly. It simply didn't matter. All that mattered was that we were together. And all these years, that's *all* that's mattered. Nothing else."

A troublesome doubt began to grow in my mind. "What do you mean, nothing else?"

"Just that. You want to know where Mom goes at Christmas? Well, so do I. I'd love to know. But I don't. And it doesn't matter. It's her secret."

It was my turn to be dumbfounded. "You mean….all these years…you don't know either? This isn't something you and Mom do together?"

His smile this time had a tinge of sadness to it. "No. That night by the campfire, your mother said to me, 'I will marry you and be your wife. I will gladly bear you a child. But I will have secrets, and you must not try to discover what they are. If you do, we cannot remain together. It is trust that will bind us and lack of trust that will break us. Do you understand?' I said I did, and I do. She said she would need a room in our house that would be just for her and that I could never enter."

"The room in the Tower she keeps locked."

"Yes. And she said that there would be two days each year when she would go away, and I was not to try to discover where she went or what she did."

I sat back. "Wow!" was all I could think to say. "And you never tried to go into her room or find out where she went?"

"Of course not! I gave her my word. Trust binds us; lack of trust breaks us. I wouldn't risk that."

"Did you know she would be away over Christmas?"

He shrugged. "No. I discovered that the first year we were married, just after you were born. I think she was surprised, too."

"What, she got a message, like from Santa Claus or something, telling her to report for duty at the North Pole?" I was kidding, of course; I'd stopped believing in Santa Claus years earlier. But then, suddenly, it didn't sound so fantastic, after all.

"I don't know. The first time she disappeared, when she came back, she put her fingers to my lips as I was about to ask and said, 'Remember your promise.' Then she kissed me. I've never tried to ask since."

"Wow!" I said again.

"You remember the story of the selkie," Dad asked, leaning forward.

"What? The magical seal that took off its skin and became a woman and married the fisherman? You think Mom's really a seal?"

He laughed. "No, I don't. Hey, we met in the desert, remember? No ocean there. And while I think your mom's pretty magical, I don't think she's a magical being." He paused. "But what do I know? I'm just a cosmologist. But that wasn't the point I wanted to make."

"What is the point, if you don't think Mom's a selkie?"

"It's really a story about trust. The fisherman and his wife had a good life, as long as he trusted her and didn't try to discover her secret of why she would disappear for a time. When he broke that trust, she left him."

"You think Mom would leave you if you peeked into her room?"

"No. I don't. But love is all about trust, Holly, and I'd have broken her trust. Things wouldn't be the same between us after that."

"Doesn't it bother you, this mystery about Mom? And what about Aunt Megan? Now she's disappeared, too! More mystery!"

He grinned. "Holly, I deal with mysteries every day. The universe is filled with mysteries, things I can see but I don't understand. Heck, the universe itself is a mystery. If one of those mysteries decides to love me and, I might add, give me YOU…." He lunged forward and started tickling me. Laughing and squealing, I fell off the sofa. "Then I'm going to go with it," he finished, sitting up and laughing with me. "You can't be an astronomer and a poet without having a tolerance for mysteries, and your Mom is one mystery I'm very happy to tolerate!"

He untangled himself from his blanket and got up. "Let's heat up those pancakes, kiddo. And then we'll open some packages under the tree."

Dad and I had a special Christmas that year, as if his opening up and sharing some of his feelings about Mom and her disappearances had dissolved some barrier between us. And the next day life continued on as normal as, right on schedule, I woke to find Mom and Aunt Megan chatting with Dad in the kitchen over breakfast as if nothing at all had happened.

But something *had* happened, inside me if not outwardly. Dad's story about his meeting with Mom had given me some information I hadn't had before, but it hadn't answered my big questions. If anything, it had intensified them. Who was this woman who could appear and disappear seemingly at will, showing up in the middle of the desert with no apparent means of transport, vanishing from her home every Christmas Eve day without luggage or even a taxi showing up, much less Dad taking her somewhere? And now, apparently, she had a sister who could do the same thing? Really? What was going on?

The mystery at the heart of our family had been nicely balanced all the years of my growing up, its strangeness countered by the obvious love my parents had for each other and for me, and by Mom's overflowing joy in the awesomeness of life and the world around her. There were so many good things about our lives that this one thing, this unexplained and unexplainable thing, could be overlooked, even folded into the magic of our household.

Aunt Megan's arrival changed this for me. When it had just been Mom, I'd learned to live with the mystery and accept it. But now I discovered she had a sister who could disappear with her.

This was too much. Just who were they? What were they?

I wanted to just ask Mom, the way I had Dad. But I didn't. I couldn't. Something stopped me. For the first time in my life, I felt distant from my mother. The mystery stood between us.

I didn't like it.

I thought of talking with Aunt Megan, but the way she had put me off that day in Mom's art room made me suspect she'd be no more forthcoming than my mother.

So, I brooded in the weeks following Christmas. My imagination began to run wild. Were my mother and her sister aliens disguised as humans? Were they faerie beings like in Dad's story about the selkie? If so, then what did that make me? Who was I?

It's hard enough about to become a teenager. Thinking I might not even be human was too much. I decided I had to do something about this.

I was sure that if I confessed my fears to my parents, they would laugh at first, then they would be sympathetic and supportive, ending up by saying as they always did, "When you're old enough," as if that solved everything. I needed to take direct action, and I knew exactly what it had to be.

I had to get into the forbidden room.

I looked up on the Internet how to pick locks. No need to go to burglar school. I found several websites and YouTube videos that showed me just how to do it. All I needed was one of my bobby pins! My own little lockpick, close at hand!

All the doors of the rooms in our house had locks, though we never used them. A little investigating showed me that the lock on the forbidden room was the same as the lock on my bedroom door. This gave me opportunities to practice. I would lock my door and then try to open it by picking the lock with a bobby pin. It proved easier to do than I'd thought. Whole new career opportunities were opening up before me!

I wondered why, if Mom's room were so special, it didn't

have a special lock. Then I realized that the true lock wasn't the one in the door but the one in Dad's heart. It was trust. She trusted him not to go into that room, so he didn't. He'd made her a promise, one he would never break.

But I hadn't made any promises. Mom assumed that I wouldn't try to sneak into her forbidden room. She'd deflected my questions about it. She simply had told me not to go in there, and for years, that was enough for me. But she'd never actually asked for my promise not to do so. I had no vows to break.

Yet, having made up my mind to go into that room and having gained the means to do so, bobby pin in hand, I kept putting it off. I kept making excuses to myself. Mom or Megan were always there in the art room (which wasn't true, but it still made a good excuse). I had to study. I was too busy. I had shopping expeditions with my girlfriends. There was always something.

Finally, I confronted myself one evening lying in bed. Why was I putting it off? I realized I was frightened of what I might find. What if Mom really was an alien? Would that make me an alien, too? What would that mean? Did I want to know?

I also realized that though I'd never actually promised Mom not to go into her room, there was still an implied trust there that I wouldn't. She had asked me not to. Love is trust, Dad had said, and Mom, knowing I loved her, assumed that I would trust her as well. And I did. I really did. In many ways, Mom was my best friend. I would die before I would hurt her.

But I had to know. This had gone on too long. I had to know the mystery at the heart of our family, and the room seemed to contain the answers.

I was afraid to know.

This conflict continued through the summer and into the autumn. I dithered and dathered. My resolve would rise, then it would sink.

I realize I'm making it sound like this problem consumed me. It didn't. We had plenty of good times, my family and I. Mom and

I would still take periodic mother-daughter picnics out into the desert where we would exclaim over the beauty of wildflowers or over seeing a kangaroo rat hopping about on its large hind feet.

There was one day, on one of our outings when she told me about the ocean that had once covered the desert millions of years ago. "All this," she said, spinning about with her arms sweeping out, "was once on the bottom of the sea!" She laughed then, running about and making swimming motions as if she were some sea creature. It suddenly brought back to mind Dad's story about the selkie who shed her skin. Crazily, I wondered if Mom had another skin somewhere around here in the desert.

Maybe that was what was behind the forbidden door. Her second skin.

For a couple of hours that day, my resolve to break into that room and see for myself was strong. I determined I would do it that night when everyone was asleep. But by the time we got home, where Aunt Megan had dinner ready for us, I'd come up with more excuses putting it off.

A month before Christmas, I had my thirteenth birthday. I was now officially a teenager. There was a special breakfast and then, in the afternoon and evening, a party with friends and cake and games and presents. It was wonderfully fun, but throughout the day, I kept waiting for something. Finally, I realized I was waiting for Mom to say to me, "Now you're old enough, and I can tell you where I go every Christmas!" But she never did.

The day before Christmas Eve Day, I was in the kitchen helping Aunt Megan bake a large batch of cookies that Dad and I planned to take to a homeless shelter on Christmas Day. Mom came in from doing some chores elsewhere in the house and began to help.

"I guess you and Aunt Megan are going to go away again tomorrow?" I asked, my hands in a bowl of dough. I was feeling a bit grumpy, but my moods had been going up and down anyway.

Mom smiled. "Yes. But it's just for a couple of days."

"But one of them's Christmas Day, Mom! Can't you stay for once?"

"No, but we'll be back after Christmas Day. We'll celebrate together then, just as we always do."

"But...But where do you go? Can't you tell me that at least?"

"I *will* tell you, Holly, when you're old enough."

The dreaded words. This time they were like oil poured on slumbering embers, causing a fire to erupt. Rage coursed through me, so strong that I couldn't speak. Thirteen wasn't old enough? My hands still covered in dough, I turned and stomped out of the kitchen and to my room where I slammed the door shut and locked it. When Mom came by later and knocked, I wouldn't let her in. "Go away," I said. "Come back when I'm old enough!"

I sulked in my room the rest of the day. I cried some, but mostly I was burning with anger. I was being denied something I felt I had to have, something I had to know.

Eventually, I fell asleep.

The next morning, I stayed in my room, telling Dad I wasn't hungry when he shouted from the kitchen that breakfast was ready. Mom may have told him I was in a bad mood before she left as he didn't press me to come or try to jolly me up. He just left me alone. Finally, around noon, I came out, driven by hunger. Dad fixed a big lunch of tacos and enchiladas, one of my favorite meals. Then we went into Tucson to see a movie and have dinner.

When we got home, it was way after dark. We stayed up awhile watching some Christmas Eve special on TV, during which Dad fell asleep on the sofa. I roused him enough to tell him to go to bed, which he did, leaving me sitting alone in the living room to finish watching the program.

It hit me that now was the time. If I was ever going to break into the forbidden room and see what was there, it had to be now. Now, while Mom was gone. Now, before Christmas Day itself. Now, now, now…. It was like a chant pulsing through my blood.

Almost in a trance, I got up and went into my room where I got my trusty bobby pin. Then it was across the living room, through the kitchen, and into the door that led to the Tower. Up one flight of stairs. Then a second, and I was standing in front of Mom's darkened art room.

I didn't turn on the light. I think some part of me felt guilty about what I was about to do and didn't want to be seen doing it, even though no one was about. I walked through the room, past the tables strewn with the art projects Mom and Aunt Megan were doing. Mom always said that everything in the room was alive. If so, if felt as if all that life were holding its breath, waiting to see what was about to happen. It felt as if the whole world were balancing on a pinhead, about to fall one way or another.

I reached the locked door and took a deep breath. Could I do it, now that I was actually here? Apparently so, for almost as if another will had taken hold, my hands reached out and began manipulating the lock with the bobby pin.

I felt the lock click.

I grasped the knob and turned.

The door opened.

And there it was. For the first time ever, I stood in the doorway of the forbidden room

It was empty.

I can't begin to describe what I felt at that moment. Shock, disappointment, anger, bewilderment…they were all there. This was Mom's big secret? An empty walk-in closet? Why was it forbidden? What was in here—or had been in here—that was so valuable, so precious, so…so *Mom's* that Dad and I had been barred from seeing it?

I felt a thrill of anger at what felt like thirteen years of deception, a cruel joke on Mom's part. Maybe she really was a crazy woman. Some of my friends thought so, even though they loved her craziness.

But there was still the mystery of where Mom was. And Aunt Megan, too.

I was about to close the door and go to bed when I realized that the room wasn't entirely empty. At the back of the room, in the shadows, there was something.

I went back and turned on the lights in the art room. Returning to the forbidden closet, I could now see that at the rear of the little room was a large wardrobe.

"Oh no," I muttered as I walked up to it. "You're not going all Narnia on me, are you, Mom?"

I opened the wardrobe door.

Inside, there was no magical portal leading to another world. Only the back side of the wardrobe. But there *was* something hanging on the clothes rod. At first, I couldn't make out what it was.

Then I did.

It was skin. Human skin, hanging loose on a hanger as if it were some costume to be worn and then taken off.

I wanted to scream, but my throat shut from fear. All I could do was gurgle. Dad was right, I thought. Mom *is* a selkie, or something, and this is her skin.

Mom always said I was her brave little girl, but right then, I felt anything but. Still, amazingly, I reached out to touch the skin-suit hanging there. It was warm and soft, just like human flesh. This time, I really wanted to scream, but I didn't. There was nothing gory about it, no blood, no bits of tissue hanging out here and there, just warm skin in the shape of a person. A person, I suddenly realized with a relief so profound that my legs almost collapsed under me, that did not have my mother's face. Whoever or whatever owned this skin, it wasn't Mom.

Then I recognized it was Aunt Megan. The skin suit had her face and hair.

This time, I did scream. I slammed the wardrobe shut, ran out of the closet-room, slammed its door shut behind me, and ran all the way to my room. There, I locked the door behind me, jumped into bed, and pulled the covers over my head. And waited for the Megan-Thing, the Thing that Wore Megan's Skin, to come get me.

It was then, lying in bed, hiding under the covers, that I realized I wasn't afraid. Not really. I was shocked. I was surprised. I was bewildered and confused by what I'd seen. However, though I'd been acting like a screaming heroine in a bad horror movie, I wasn't afraid. From somewhere deep within me, I felt a wave of peacefulness arising. The skin suit wasn't Mom, so whatever or wherever she was, she wasn't a skin-shedding monster. She was Mom, and I trusted her love. I had no idea what was happening, but from that deep, hitherto unknown place inside me, everything felt unexplainably right.

Filled with wonderment about this, I fell asleep.

I was awakened by a silvery light filling my room. Opening my eyes and blinking into the light, I saw a figure standing by my bed. As my eyes focused, I realized it was Mom. She looked just as she always did, skin and all, except that she was glowing with this silvery light.

"Mom!" I cried, sitting up.

Smiling, she reached out and pulled me out of the bed, helping me to stand up.

"Come with me," she said. She put a finger gently to my lips. "But do not talk."

I was bursting with questions, but this shut me up. I followed her out of my bedroom, down the hall, and into the living room where, according to our family tradition, the lights on the Christmas tree were lit and bright. The silvery light around my mother outshone them all, as if the full moon itself had stepped into the room.

We walked on in silence into the kitchen, and I knew we were retracing my steps towards the forbidden room. Up the Tower stairs we went, into the art room and beyond it into the room that had held my curiosity for so many years and had been the object of so many fantasies. The room that had proven to be empty.

Only now it was not empty. In the middle of the room was a silvery staircase. It seemed to sparkle as if embedded with millions of tiny diamonds or even stars. It led up to the ceiling and seemed to merge into it.

We stood in the little room for a moment, Mom seemingly lost in thought, me gazing in wonder at this staircase that had most certainly not been there earlier in the evening. Mom looked at me and said matter-of-factly, "You were in here earlier."

Not daring to speak and feeling guilty, I nodded.

She nodded back. "I thought so. I felt you here. It drew me back." She sighed. "I thought it was too soon, that you weren't yet old enough. But you have the blood, and it would not wait. It heard the Call and had to respond."

What call? I wanted to ask, but Mom turned away and started up the staircase. I followed right behind her. When we reached the ceiling, which was only a few steps up, we passed through it as if it weren't there.

I thought we might emerge into some other realm, but instead, the staircase ended on the roof of the Tower, the normal roof where Dad had his telescope and where Mom and I would lie on blankets, looking up at the stars. Taking my hand, Mom stepped off onto the roof with me beside her.

I saw that we were not alone. Another figure shared the roof with us. Like Mom, it glowed with a silvery light but its light was brighter. It had a human shape, but the face was featureless—or else I just couldn't make out the features that were there, obscured by the glow around its head. Nevertheless, something in me knew that this figure was Aunt Megan.

Aunt Megan without her skin.

The figure came over and hugged me. I felt suffused in love

and calm. "Holly," it said, and it was Aunt Megan's voice.

Filled with wonder, I almost missed Mom saying, "Now we wait."

Wait? I wondered. *Wait for what?*

I did not have long to wonder, though. I felt something in me, I could not have told you what, rise up and reach out, as if some part of me was yearning towards the stars. I saw Mom look up. I did the same. In the distance, a bright light was heading towards us, as if a star had detached itself from the night sky and was falling earthward. No, I realized, not falling. Flying, and heading in our direction.

As it drew closer, I finally was able to see what it was. I couldn't believe my eyes. It was a golden sleigh being pulled by four, large snowy owls, like something out of Harry Potter. Riding in the sleigh was a woman garbed in white, long white hair billowing behind her like a cloak as she flew. The whole ensemble glowed with the same silvery light that was around my mother, only many times brighter.

This is impossible, I thought. Then I realized that on this night of all nights, Christmas Eve, with my mother and aunt both shining like the moon itself, "impossible" had no meaning.

The owl-pulled sleigh stopped right by the edge of the roof of the Tower, magically defying gravity as it hovered in the air, the owls' wings folded against their bodies. The woman in white looked at us. She was inhumanly beautiful. I had no idea how old she was. She seemed ageless, youthful in appearance, but with eyes that seemed to hold a million years or more of wisdom and experience. Something deep in me, unknown to me until this moment, spoke, and my lips formed the word.

"Mother."

And I didn't mean Mom.

The woman smiled at the three of us and asked of my mother, "Is it her time?"

"I didn't think so," my mother replied. "She has yet to come into her womanhood. But her blood heard the call and would not be put off longer."

The woman looked at me. "Do you wish to ride with us?"

I didn't even think about it. "Oh yes, Mother," I said. "Oh yes!"

"Then take my hand." The woman clothed in white extended a pale hand to me, and I held it. A heartbeat later, I was on the sleigh, sitting in the back with Mom on one side of me and the being I knew as Aunt Megan on the other. I was surrounded by light, even glowing myself as if my blood had turned to starlight. I was flying through the air, the snowy owls beating their silent, powerful wings before us.

This can't be real, I thought to myself, as we soared over the land, swooping low over neighborhoods. *I must be dreaming.*

No, you're not. It was Mom's voice, but I was hearing her in my mind, not with my ears. *It's real. And you're safe.* I felt unseen arms around me and knew they were my mother's.

Another voice spoke in my mind. My body thrummed to its power. *Let me speak with her, Daughter.*

My mother's voice, softer but, I realized, born of the same power, replied. *As you wish.*

I didn't move but suddenly, I found myself in the front of the sleigh next to the woman in white. Magic. Of course.

"Welcome, Daughter, to your first Ride," she said, speaking out loud, glancing at me next to her.

"Ride?" I asked,

The woman laughed. The sound made me want to laugh, too, as if we were sharing a joke with the universe and all the stars were laughing with us. "Yes. Men have their Wild Hunt, so let us call this, the Awful Ride!"

"I don't understand," I said.

"I am Mother Awe," she said. "We ride to bring Awe into the world. Look back."

I turned to look over my shoulder behind me. I could see the light from the sleigh spreading out like a comet's tail, turning into a mist that descended onto the homes below.

I looked back at the woman beside me, her face regal in profile as she looked ahead. "That light is…is awe?"

"The awe is in the hearts of those below, waiting to be reawakened. The light calls them to remember and to see the world with the awe it deserves." She looked at me. "People are forgetting. The world may seem awesome to them, but not awful, full of awe. If it were, they would not treat it as they do. They would not ignore the life that surrounds them in all that is. They would love the world, as I do."

I thought about this for a moment. If anyone saw the world as full of awe, it was Mom. "My Mom sees awe," I said out loud. "She sees wonder everywhere, in everything. Is that why she's here, on this Ride?"

"Yes, but this is not the only reason, Daughter. Your mother comes from the Star-Born, as do you, and the Star-Born carry Awe in their very blood. Truly, they are the People of Awe."

"Comes from the Star-Born?" I thought of the human skin hanging in the wardrobe at home. "Are you saying Mom is an alien? I'm an alien?"

The woman laughed again. "All life is kin. No life is alien to other life," she said, which I felt didn't really answer my question. As if sensing my confusion, she added, "There are those who are beings of starlight and energy. At times they are able to wear a human skin and step from their world into yours. They may even mate with a human, and when they do, their children may be like your mother."

"You mean, someone like Aunt Megan, Mom's sister…"

Mother Awe looked at me oddly, then laughed. "Her sister? Is that what she told you? Child, she is your grandmother."

"My grandmother!"

Before I could begin to process this, the sleigh suddenly

banked to the right as the owls made a sharp turn, tipping on its side as it did. I cried out in surprise and gripped the edge of the sleigh to keep from falling out. But something held me in place.

"You cannot fall," said the woman. "Things are not as they seem. Tell me, what do you see?"

"I'm on a sleigh drawn by four owls flying through the night sky on Christmas Eve." I still couldn't believe it even as I said it.

She laughed. "How delightful! Now see what I see." She reached over, a pale hand touching my forehead. Everything changed. The land below, the sky above, the sleigh around me, even the woman herself, all disappeared. Instead, I was floating in a sphere of misty Light. I sensed rather than saw the earth below me, completely enveloped by this sphere. Everything was still, and yet I had an impression of vibrant activity all around me.

"We are outside your time and space, Daughter. We are everywhere and nowhere. We are flying over your land, and we are flying over all lands. Who can say where we are? We are the cloud of Awe that covers the earth."

I remembered a day when Dad and I were watching a science show on television. The atom was being presented as a tiny solar system, with the electrons spinning madly around the nucleus like planets around the sun. Dad had said that was wrong, that the electrons were really like a cloud around the nucleus. "It's called Uncertainty," he'd said. "An electron could be anywhere in that cloud. You can't measure it exactly."

That was what I was seeing now. Awe was a cloud around the earth, and the sleigh was one expression of it in time and space.

But I was Holly, a real girl of flesh and blood. How could I be everywhere at once, and myself, too? It made my head hurt to think about it.

I was suddenly back in the sleigh. "It's better that you see it this way, Daughter," the woman said. "You are not ready for the multidimensional side of the world, or of yourself, yet." I had to agree. Incredible as a flying sleigh pulled by owls was, it was more understandable than the *everywhereness* I'd just experienced.

Then I had a thought. "This is like Santa, isn't it? Santa's a cloud, too, just like we are."

The woman looked over at me, her eyebrows lifted in surprise. "This is perceptive of you. Yes, the Mystery that you call Santa Claus is also a quality that surrounds the world, able to be both here and everywhere." She frowned. "His 'cloud,' as you call it, is much diminished, though. It has been squeezed into mortal concepts of commerce that have left him a pale imitation of all he could be in the daily lives of men and women. He is bound to one night and thought of as a myth for children." She snorted. "Mortals are foolish to dismiss the Mysteries, so. Your world much needs what we can bring."

I was busy re-evaluating my own thoughts about Santa, having dismissed him as a 'myth for children' myself when she added, "He still has one power, though. The thought of him opens hearts this night, which is why our Ride is important now and tomorrow. He makes the ground more fertile for the Awe we bring."

"This is why Mom disappears every Christmas. She's riding with you."

"Yes. Many ride with me, Daughter. All women share our cloud, for it is in women to know the awe of life. But those who come from the Star-Born, they are a bridge between our world and yours. Their presence in the sleigh gives us added power these special nights."

I looked back. "But there's only Mom and my... my *grandmother* back there."

The woman in white smiled at me. "Have you not learned not to trust your eyes here?"

Something shifted again in my mind, and suddenly, a multitude of women were there, all around us, in the sleigh, beside the sleigh, part of the sleigh, part of the Cloud of Awe. Some were like my Aunt Megan, Star-Born. Others were like Mom, and, I

Mother Awe

suddenly realized, like me, women born of a Star-Born. And others were women fully human but holding in their hearts love for the world, women whose spirits could link with Mother Awe on her starlit ride, even though their bodies slept in beds or were busy with the chores of life. Women who could join us in bringing awe to the world because awe lived in them.

Unable to take it all in, I closed my eyes. I bent my head and began to cry with the wonder and joy of it but also for a world that was parched and thirsty for the touch of Awe.

I felt a gentle touch on my shoulder. "Your mother says this is enough for your first Ride. I agree. We shall take you home."

"Take me home?" I asked, brushing away tears and taking a breath. "The cloud is everywhere, isn't it? You don't need to take me back anywhere. We're already there, aren't we?"

She laughed. "Yes, but I fear you have had enough of the cloud. We shall fly home the old-fashioned way, through time and space."

I settled back into the softness of the seat. As I relaxed, a thought came to me. I looked over at Mother Awe and said, "I would like the secret between my mother and father to end. I would like him to know where Mom goes on Christmas and what she does."

She frowned. "This is not possible, child."

"Why? Why is it not possible?"

"Because he is a man."

"Really?" I said. I couldn't believe it. Mother Awe was a feminist? "Why should that make a difference?"

There was coldness in her voice as she replied. "I told you. Men have their Wild Hunt. They celebrate conquest and death. They have abandoned the way of life. They have made the world something dead, without wonder, without awe, a thing to be used."

"Not all men," I said. "Not my father." But it was as if she

31

hadn't heard me.

"The Awful Ride is women's Ride. Men have stripped awe from the world. If they knew of the Ride, they would diminish it as well. They would do to me what they have done to Santa Claus, turning the Mystery of Giving and Joy into a one-night stand meant only for children."

"No," I said.

She snorted, turning her face away from me. "You are too young. You are not yet a woman. You do not know. The Ride brings power to women, a power that men fear. They hate what they fear and will take it away, as they have in the past."

"My father wouldn't! He didn't ever try to find out how Mom mysteriously appeared to him in the desert when they first met!" A thought suddenly came to me. "She came out of the stars, didn't she? Made a body for herself that night on the desert, just like… like my grandmother."

"No. Your mother is not Star-Born that way. But she can walk the secret paths the stars weave around the earth."

Walk secret star-paths? The thought thrilled me. I really wanted to do *that*. But I was not to be put off. "Whatever," I said. "The point is that all these years, he's let her have her secrets. He has let her have her mysteries." I thought this was an important point that would make my case. She didn't agree.

"Your father is not like most men."

Angry, I swept my arms out. "So, all this, the Sleigh, the cloud, the Mystery, it's only for women? The Awe that you spread, only women can receive it? Is this what you're saying?"

Her voice softened, but she refused to look at me. "For now. In time, men can know, but not now. Not until women are strong again, strong in their power, strong in their Awe and the Ride cannot be stopped."

I couldn't believe what I was hearing. Even more, I couldn't believe what I said next. Who was I, a newbie teenager, to challenge one of the Mysteries of the world, someone probably older than the world itself. But this is what teenagers do, isn't it? We challenge our elders!

"Then I don't want to be part of this Ride," I shouted. "Awe can't be just for women! Dad feels awe at the world as much as Mom. More than me, probably! And I know he's not alone. Men and women together must bring awe back into the world, not just women! Otherwise, this Ride is already stopped!"

There was silence.

More quietly but no less intensely, I said, "Dad says that love is all about trust. You claim to love the world, to love humanity. Then you have to trust men and women. You have to trust all of us. Together."

More silence.

"Well?" I insisted.

The woman in white turned her head, and I was surprised to see her smiling. "You have spoken to Mystery. Now, sleep." She reached out and touched my forehead for a second time. Everything disappeared.

The next thing I knew, I was opening my eyes in my own bed. The sun was not quite up, but a pre-dawn light came through my window. I lay there, disoriented. I wasn't sure where I was or even who I was. Then it all came back in a rush: the breaking into the forbidden room, Aunt Megan's skin-suit hanging in the wardrobe, my mother and me going up the magical staircase, the coming of Mother Awe, the Awful Ride, my shouting at a planetary Mystery. It had been a dream. Hadn't it? None of that could have been real. Could it?

I got up and padded into the bathroom. That's when I discovered spots of blood on my pajamas. I had bled during the night. OMG! My first period had started! I was now officially a woman.

I wandered back into my bedroom, not sure what to do, feeling scared, wondering how to tell Dad, and wishing with all my heart that Mom were there.

The door opened, and there she was.

Mom.

On Christmas Morning.

I cried out and ran into her embrace. "Mom," I cried. "You're home!"

She hugged me tightly. "Yes! I'm home. Mother Awe said I was needed here." Then she saw the blood-spotted pajama bottoms I was still carrying. "And now I know why! Holly, you've become a woman on Christmas Day! That's awesome!" She laughed with the joy of it, and I laughed with her. I was a woman! And Mom was home on Christmas!

At that moment, Aunt Megan came into the room, looking perfectly normal in what I now knew was her human skin. "Aunt…I mean…Grandmother?"

She smiled. "Yes, Granddaughter. We thought it would raise fewer questions to say I was your mother's sister rather than her mother."

I looked at her appraisingly. "You really don't look like you could be Mom's mother."

She laughed. "I was wearing a different skin when she was conceived."

I didn't know what to say to that. Overnight, my world had not only become so much larger but very weird as well.

I looked at Mom. "Does Dad know you're here?"

"No. Let's go wake him up and tell him!"

"Tell him?" I thought of my argument with Mother Awe. "You mean, everything?"

"Yes, everything!"

"But Mother Awe said…"

"I know. You changed her mind. Or maybe it was just a test, to see what you thought. Who knows the mind or reasons of one of the Mysteries."

"So, I can Ride with you next year?"

She laughed. "Yes. *Now*, you're old enough!"

I changed into fresh pajamas, then we went down the hall as quietly as we could to the door to Mom and Dad's bedroom. Before we opened it to rush in shouting Merry Christmas, I whispered to Mom, "Maybe next year, Dad will go on the Ride with us, too."

She smiled back. "I have no doubt about it!"

THE BAILEY

The little bell above the door tinkled as the boy opened it and ran out, clutching the book tightly to his chest. As if in echo, before the door closed, I could hear from down the street the sound of the Salvation Army's Santa Claus, ringing for donations.

"He didn't pay for it, did he?"

I could hear the resigned sigh hiding behind the words. I turned to face Mary, my store manager and absolutely essential bookkeeper. She was frowning, and I knew she'd been spending the last hour working out our profit and loss statement for the end of the year.

I grinned. "No, he didn't."

"And you think he'll read it?" Mary would never say it out loud, but I could hear the unspoken comment, *in this neighborhood?*

"I hope so," I said. "He was certainly excited about it."

"John...."

I held up my hands to forestall what was an all-too familiar conversation. "I know. I'm driving us into bankruptcy, giving books away."

This time the sigh was audible. "Not yet, John. But if you keep on...." She happened to still have the ledger book in her hand, and she shook it at me. "Figures don't lie, Boss. We're barely breaking even..."

"But we *are* breaking even, aren't we? A little profit, even... maybe?"

For a moment, the frown disappeared. "A little," she admitted. Then the frown came back, obviously enjoying its place on her forehead. "*Very* little, John. Gone in an instant when I demand my Christmas bonus."

"A demand that shall be happily and abundantly met," I said. "In fact..." I reached into a pocket in my sweater and pulled out a check. "By coincidence, I just happened to have this lurking here." I handed it to her.

"Omigosh, Boss!" she exclaimed, looking at the check in my hand. "I was just kidding." She took it. Her eyes widened as she opened it and looked at what I had written on it. "Now your profit is most definitely gone! Especially if you have one of these for Stanley!"

"Well, as a matter of fact, I do," I said, patting the same pocket. "And before you say anything more, this isn't coming out of the store's account. This is my gift to you two out of my personal funds. I couldn't run this place without both of you!"

"Be that as it may, you don't have unlimited funds in your account, either!"

At that point, there was a loud shout and much laughter from the back room where Stanley, my other employee, was running a role playing adventure for some of the neighborhood kids.

"Sounds like they're having fun......" I started to say, looking toward the back, but then the door bell tinkled again. I turned to see who had entered, and saw that it was the Eddie, the beat cop. He stood for a moment brushing some snow off his uniform, then came towards me, a wry smile on his face.

"Hello, John," said Eddie. "Merry Christmas."

"You, too, Eddie," I replied. "What brings you here? Looking for a book?" I grinned, but I had a resigned feeling that I already knew why he had come.

"Sorry, John. I wish. I'm just the bearer of bad tidings. We got another noise complaint from Mr. Abernathy. He says there's too much racket coming from, and I quote, 'your hoodlums.'" As if on cue, there was another series of loud shouts from the back room.

I sighed. "Mary, go have Stanley have the kids keep it down, will you?" As she headed off to the backroom, I said to Eddie, "It's just kids having fun, you know. In a way, it's their Christmas present to Mr. Abernathy. He's never happier than when he has something to complain about!"

Eddie chuckled. "You got that right! This is the fifth complaint he's made this week, and it's only Wednesday! Fr'nstance, he wants me to tell Mrs. Drake to turn off the Christmas display in her shop window because its lights bother him. He's the bane of the neighborhood. The holidays drive him nuts. I tell you, I think he's Scrooge incarnated."

"Well, make Scrooge forty pounds overweight, and you're probably right." I laughed. "He even came in yesterday to tell me to turn off the Christmas music in the store because he couldn't stand the noise." Abernathy's dry cleaning store shared a wall with my bookstore. "I told him to buy some ear plugs, that I wasn't going to deny my customers a bit of Christmas cheer and that I'd be happy to buy him some ear plugs as a Christmas present."

"Good for you! What did he say?"

"You know, he just frowned and stalked out, but I swear I heard him muttering 'humbug' under his breath."

Eddie laughed. "Well, OK, I've delivered the message. What you do with it is up to you. After all, it's your store, and you're hardly creating a public nuisance. If anything, it's wonderful you're giving these kids a place to go and something to do instead of hanging out on the streets."

"Thanks, Eddie. Oh, before you go, will you do me the honor of picking out a book you'd like? When I was growing up, it was the custom to give our neighborhood beat cop a present or two to say thank you."

He shook his head. "Different times now, John. We can't accept gifts. People might think you're bribing me...especially old you-know-who next door."

I shrugged. "Sad times, then. But you could always come back as a private citizen, out of uniform and all. If a book found its way into your pocket, I wouldn't call it shoplifting and call the cops."

He grinned. "I'll think about it. Thanks, John. And don't

worry about Abernathy. You keep doing what you're doing, and I'll run interference." He turned and went out onto the street, where the snow was starting to fall even harder. We had four days to go until Christmas, but it looked like it was going to be a very white one…well, as white as it could get in the middle of the city.

I thought about Abernathy. He was a dried-up, curmudgeonly old sourpuss, no doubt about it, but at one time he must have had dreams and known happiness. I knew he'd been married but, so the neighborhood gossip went, his wife had divorced him and left town, taking their daughter with her. A hard blow for any man, but if he'd been as critical and selfish then as he was now, I could understand why she'd done it.

"Maybe I can get some soundproofing material to put on the wall back there…"

"What did you say?" It was Mary, who had come up behind me and heard me muttering to myself.

I turned towards her. "Oh, I was just thinking of ways of soundproofing the backroom," I said.

"That's not your responsibility, John. You're way too accommodating to people, especially people like him."

"Well, he *is* my neighbor. You know what the Good Book says about loving neighbors. And it costs me nothing to make his life a little easier."

"Ha! It'll cost you whatever the contractor charges to put up a soundproof wall between the backroom and his store."

"No. It will just cost me the materials. Heck, I might even get someone to donate them. And I'll get the kids to do the work. It will give them good training. I know a carpenter who can oversee the project for free."

Mary threw up her hands. "Sometimes I wonder if I'm managing a bookstore or a social services center."

"A bit of both, I'd say."

"Well, then, I'd better get back to it. Oh, Stanley said to tell you it was feeding time." Mary walked over to her desk which was not far behind the front counter. That way, if I wasn't here, she could easily get up to serve a customer.

"Right. Can't have hungry gamers, can we?" Every day, I offered a hot meal in the backroom, usually lunch but sometimes on weekends, it might be dinner. But it wasn't free. The kids had to earn their food, and they did so by taking part in some activity that Stanley, Mary or I organized. It might be by participating in a role playing game, taking a reading or art class, even doing a service project somewhere in the neighborhood after school or on a weekend.

I have to admit, the role playing games were my favorite activity, though I had gladly turned over the organizing duties to Stanley. It wasn't just that, unlike Mary or me, he was closer in age to the kids, being in his early twenties. It was that he was a natural born storyteller. He excelled at being a game master, weaving exciting and complex adventures that kept the kids enthralled and coming back. No easy task with these youngsters, most of whom came from dysfunctional or broken homes. They lived with life and death on the street at a time when most kids in America were playing video games or worrying about how they appeared on social media. Capturing and keeping these kids attention was a skill that Stanley seemed to have in abundance.

There was, however, one unbreakable rule I had set down about the games. They could not be oriented to violence. These kids lived with violence as part of their daily lives. Rather the games needed to enable them to participate in a world of hope, something there wasn't a lot of in their everyday lives. There could be combat, but there needed to be positive values woven into the experience as well: values of courage, companionship, trust, and compassion. The players might balk at this rule at first—"Fantasy is for kids, man!" one of them had said when he was starting out— but it was Stanley's gift that he could draw them into a world of knighthood and honor and make it relevant to their own world.

I looked forward to the novels he would someday write!

As I went through the door into the backroom, I saw six kids clustered around the large gaming table, dice, paper, pencils, miniatures, and other role playing paraphernalia scattered about in front of them. No one spared me a glance. Their eyes—and ears—were glued on Stanley.

"You descend the worn, ancient steps into the cavern, the sound of your steps echoing around you. You know no one has been in this place since the fall of the Tavenise Empire at least a thousand years ago, but there is no dust anywhere. Everything is carved out of a white stone, and it's as clean as if it had just been washed."

"Magic," one of the kids whispered, a boy whose name was Clarence.

"Yes," said Stanley. "Magic. Holy magic! The best kind!" He looked up at me and grinned. "Well, almost the best kind. For here comes our fearless leader, bringing with him pizza magic!"

The four boys and two girls looked up at me and in one breath, all cheered. "All right," Stanley said. "Food break!"

"Can't we find out what's in the cavern?" asked one of the girls.

"Oh, we will," Stanley said, smiling. "But food first."

The backroom is really three rooms. The large room is for games, but off to the right of it is a small kitchen, really just a narrow counter with a couple of drawers for silverware, a sink, a microwave, and a small fridge and freezer. Next to it is a small storage room. As the kids broke into excited conversation about the adventure they were on, Stanley came over to help me in the kitchen.

"Sounds like they're having fun," I said, taking the pizzas out of the freezer. Stanley helped me unwrap them. "Oh, yes, Boss," he said. "Me, too. We're about to enter the ancient initiation chamber of a sacred order of knights not seen in this world for over a thousand years. The kids don't know it, but they're about find something very special."

"Really?" I popped one of the pizzas into the microwave. "Can you tell me?"

"Sorry, he said, shaking his head while collecting plates and silverware. "I don't even know myself, not really. Hey, John, you know how I work. Pure inspiration. Why don't you stay and listen? That way we can both find out!" He grinned.

"Maybe I will. Let me go let Mary know, and I'll be back."

I left Stanley preparing the pizzas and went out to the front of the store, where, to my delight, Mary was serving a couple of customers. I waited until she had finished, then I told her Stanley had invited me to sit in on the game. "He's strutting his stuff," I said. "High wire act, no notes. Making everything up as he goes along. Amazing!"

"Yes, he is that," she said. "I'm pretty sure I can handle anything here. Not that many people out now, with the snow and all. If it gets too busy, I'll just ring the bell and you can come help. Meantime, enjoy yourself! Tell me if he falls, though I'd be surprised if he did. I've been with him on a couple of his adventures."

"That's a deal."

I returned to the backroom where the gamers were all happily scarfing down pizza and drinking juice. I refused to give them sodas. Hot dogs, chips, pizza, those were OK during a Saturday gaming session like today, but I figured they got enough sugar into them at other times without me adding to it. Most of the meals I provided were designed to be pretty nutritious. In the coming year, I'd arranged with a friend of mine who had a restaurant a couple of blocks away to offer cooking lessons to anyone who wanted them. Like Mary said, I really *was* running a kind of social services center with the help of many neighborhood friends. Given all the funding cuts in the current political climate, somebody had to step in to help.

I grabbed myself a slice of pizza and a glass of water and

settled down in a chair in a corner of the room. I wanted to be as unobtrusive as possible when Stanley started up again. But he came over and squatted beside me. "You're welcome at the table, Boss," he said.

"Nah. I'd rather be out of the line of fire. Say, speaking of that, how did it go last night?" Friday nights were free movie nights here. We rarely had fewer than twenty or so show up. Stanley was master of that event, too.

"Went just fine. I showed them *It's a Wonderful Life.*"

"And they liked it?" I asked, incredulous. For some reason, I'd never enjoyed that movie, however much I liked Jimmy Stewart. I think it's because my mom and dad loved it and had my sister and me watch it every year when I was growing up. After awhile, any movie will turn sour if you see it too many times. It had become way too sappy for me.

"Looovvvved it," Stanley said, drawing out the word. "Everyone was cheering at the end." He stood up. "Thanks for asking, Boss," he said. "Well, time to get back to work. Ancient mysteries await."

In five minutes, the kids had everything cleaned up and were back at the table. I was interested to note there was a palpable shift in the atmosphere in the room as Stanley took his seat and cleared his throat. Everyone knew magic was about to happen.

"Where we we?" he asked, as if he didn't know. The girl who hadn't wanted to stop for food said, "We entering the lost, ancient chamber deep under the mountains."

"Ah yes. You step into the chamber, your breath quiet. There's a stillness in this room, an expectancy, as if this place has been waiting for you for centuries."

As Stanley described the chamber and led the gamers deeper into it, I was amazed to feel that stillness he'd described come over this backroom as well. He was creating an atmosphere, and the room was responding. Along the edges, I could feel energy gathering.

Though I wouldn't share this with just anyone, I've been in a number of magical ceremonies myself over the years. Real magical ceremonies, run by very competent operative mages who had studied and learned over many years. I'd been initiated into a magical lodge when I was in my thirties, twenty years earlier. I daresay I knew my way around the subtle energies that permeate the world, all unknown to most people in our society. And what I felt building up in the backroom of my modest little storefront bookstore was equal to anything I'd felt in any of the ceremonies I'd attended. To say that this made my antennae perk up would be an understatement.

As far as I knew, Stanley had no real background in that very misunderstood art and science that goes by the name of "magic." As someone who had been a practitioner in the past, I think I would have felt that connection in his aura. Someone who does real magic leaves traces in their energy field, and if they do a lot of it, those traces become grooves that another practitioner cannot miss. I knew that I had such grooves myself. And I was very sure that neither Mary nor Stanley knew of them or suspected that I had ever been anything other than a successful businessman who had made a modest fortune, retired, and was now running a bookstore mainly as a hobby and as an instrument for giving something back to the community. As I said, today's political climate was a harsh one, and it made it dangerous to stand out as someone somehow "different" than everyone else.

I pulled my wandering thoughts back to the events going on around the gaming table. Stanley had led the group to an altar of gleaming white stone. Shaped like an upright egg, it balanced perfectly upon a pedestal. Threads of gold ran down the sides of the egg from its point to its base, and above the point, a silver flame hovered in the air, giving out light but no heat. Goose bumps ran up and down my arms. *My god*, I thought, *I'd seen that altar in dreams.*

"You form a circle around this altar. Then, you kneel before it," Stanley said, and I suddenly felt an irrational desire to leap up from the chair and kneel myself. *Steady*, I told myself. *It's just a game.* But the energy in the room was building, invoked by the oldest form of magic known to humanity: that of a talented story-teller.

"As you kneel, the altar suddenly becomes brighter. You see the silver flame expanding, growing taller and wider. It's like a door opening, and through it, you see two figures appearing in the air above the altar. They are both clad in shining, golden armor, and above their heads, a golden flame hovers, casting its light over all of you."

Omigosh, I thought. I could see these two figures appearing in the air over the gaming table. I knew they weren't there physically. None of the kids noticed them, so entranced were they—and that's exactly the right word—by Stanley's words and tone of voice. Somehow, the energy in the room had stimulated my inner sight, and I was seeing into the subtle dimension that surrounds us all. In a way that would have made any operative mage envious, Stanley had actually invoked two of the Powers that lived and worked in the spiritual dimensions of the world.

There's nothing quite as dangerous as someone working real magic without knowing what he or she is doing and without any training in the Art. I was afraid this was happening with Stanley. Somehow he was wading into deeper and deeper inner waters and taking the kids with him. I began to prepare a banishing ritual in my mind, something that would break the spell and close the portal he was, I was sure, inadvertently opening.

Then I realized as clearly as if someone had whispered it in my ears, which, given the Powers involved, perhaps someone had, that it wasn't Stanley that was doing this. These Powers were here on their own, for reasons of their own, using this game adventure and the imagination it evoked as a portal into our world. They were in control of what was happening, and all would be well.

Knowing this, I relaxed and waited to see what would

happen.

"A voice rings out through the chamber," Stanley said, and suddenly his voice grew deeper and more resonant. "Place your swords on the floor before you, hit towards the flame, point towards yourselves."

The hair rose on my arms as, nearly as one, all the kids intoned, "We place our swords as bidden."

"The male figure speaks. 'I am the Knight of Fiery Hope,' he says. The female figure speaks, 'And I am the Lady of Fiery Hope. We are what the world needs. Will you be our knights?'"

As one the kids said, "We swear it, our Lady!" I knew then that we'd left the world of the game and entered a whole other reality. Did the kids really know what they were saying?

"The Knight speaks," Stanley said. "'Will you bring hope to your world and a vision of new possibilities?'"

"We will," spoke the gamers.

"The Lady speaks. 'Will you protect the helpless, honor the truth, and shine with compassion?'"

"We will, our Lady!"

"The Knight speaks. 'Will you serve the world with kindness, helpfulness, and love?'"

"We will, Sir Knight."

I knew by then it was not the conscious minds of the kids that were speaking and answering but something much deeper. Their souls were responding, answering the Powers that had entered the room.

"You watch in awe," Stanley continued, "as your swords rise into the air, their hilts towards the Knight and Lady of Hope, their points towards you. The Lady speaks, 'Then we anoint you as Knights of this Sacred Order. Remember, every life matters, every life deserves kindness, every life is worthy of love." A stream of Light pours out from the Knight and the Lady, running along each of your swords, and bathing you, piercing you in the heart."

I could see it happening! From the two figures hovering above the gaming table, Light shown down on each of the boys and girls, their faces rapt with wonder. I saw their auras suddenly flare with Light, and I knew, as impossible and wondrous as it seemed, that I was witnessing a true initiation. It was happening not in a temple and not in the midst of a consecrated circle of mages but over a gaming table in the backroom of a bookstore. And there had been no warning at all that this would or even could occur.

"Your swords flip over, their hilts towards you. You each grip your sword in your hand and then you rise. You rise, Sir Knights," Stanley said, "and raise your swords in honor to the Light." And as one, the gamers all physically stood up and raised their arms and hands just as if they were gripping imaginary swords now pointing not at themselves but towards the two figures of Light hovering above the table. By this point, I had no idea if they could actually see these figures or not.

"This figures salute you, then fade back into the silver flame which dwindles in size until it is as it was when you entered this chamber." As Stanley spoke, I watched as the actual figures I was seeing faded away, and I could feel the subtle energies diminishing in the room around me. "But now, you are not as you were when you entered. You have been changed. You are initiates of the Light. You are Knights of the long-forgotten, long-lost order."

"And what order is this," one of the boys asked, as they all sat down around the table again. "What is its name?"

"It is…" and Stanley paused dramatically, "the Order of the Baileys!"

"The Baileys!" The gamers shouted, and a cheer went up, along with much laughter. "Right on, man!" I heard Clarence shout at Stanley, giving him a fist bump.

The Baileys? I thought. *What the hell name of a knightly order was that?*

"Now, go forth and be a shield against the Potters." Stanley said. "That's all for today. We'll pick up next Saturday. Remember to store all your game gear in the cupboard over there."

There were some predictable moans and groans; I could see they were both reluctant to leave the magical world of the game and yet, eager to get back into their own worlds. I wondered if it was safe to let them go, given all the energy that had been directed into them, but something in me felt all was well. None of the kids seemed dangerously over-stimulated, so I figured whatever had happened, the Powers had it in hand. But just in case, I walked over to Clarence as he was putting his dice and other role playing materials in the cupboard.

"Wow, Clarence, that was some ending!"

He grinned at me. "Yeah, man, very cool. But it's just the beginning. I think Stan's got something even radder up his sleeve for next week."

"So how do you feel after that initiation?"

"Me? I feel fine. My character, he's probably shook up, you know what I mean?"

"I guess so. It would shake me up if it were happening to me."

He laughed. "Nah, I figure you'd take it in your stride, man." He punched me lightly on the shoulder and left the room. I figured he was none the worse for what had happened. But I intended to keep a close eye on the kids over the next few days, just in case.

After they all had left, I said to Stanley, "That was impressive. You really created an atmosphere with your story." I was curious how aware he'd been of what had happened.

"Yeah, Boss. The kids really got into it. They're a hard-boiled bunch out on the streets—they need to be—but go a little deeper, and they all have rich imaginations just looking for a bit of wonderment and magic."

"And you supplied that to them."

"Well, all I did was tell the story. They supplied the imaginations." And with that, I realized that he'd not been aware at all of anything extraordinary happening.

"But where did you come up with that silly name for the order of knights?" I asked. "The Order of Bailey?"

"Not silly at all, Boss," said Stanley, taking his backpack out of the cupboard. "It was something they could relate to, a way of making it all real to them."

"Really? I don't get it."

"Actually, I thought it was very clever, if I do say so. It's why I picked the movie I did last night and made sure they'd see it. I knew they'd make the connection in the game."

"The connection? I don't....oh!"

"Now you get it, don't you, Boss?"

I did, and I felt chagrined I hadn't seen it immediately. After all those years of seeing *It's a Wonderful Life,* the reference should have been right there for me, just as it was for the kids who'd seen the movie the night before. The hero of the movie is George Bailey, the head of a small savings and loan bank whose self-sacrifice and kindness keeps his hometown of Bedford Falls from falling into the clutches of Henry Potter, the richest man in town and a selfish old miser, and turning into mean-spirited Pottersville. "Well," I said, still puzzled. "I see the connection with the movie, but I still don't get why you wanted to use it in the game."

"Look, John," Stanley said, and I recognized the tone he gets in his voice when he has to patiently explain something that should be obvious, "old man Potter in the movie? The villain?" I nodded. "He's mean, selfish, only out for himself and all he can get, and has a low opinion of human beings. Well, these kids run into 'Potters' all the time, especially in this neighborhood and especially now with the way politics are in this country. Why, there are times I think the people running the show would like to turn the whole country into a Pottersville!" It was my turn to nod. Sometimes lately, I'd been fearing the same thing. "I mean, look," Stanley was continuing, obviously warming to his topic, "we've got a Potter right next door!"

I held up my hand. "Oh, I don't think Abernathy's as bad as all that! He's just an old grouch. Not quite the same thing."

"I beg to differ, Boss. But my point is these kids see Potters all around them. But…" he paused. "They see people like George Bailey, too. They understand kindness and self-sacrifice. They don't see a lot of it these days, but they recognize it. What I want is for them to recognize it in themselves."

The light dawned. "You want them to be like George Bailey."

"Bingo! Why not?" He waved an arm that took in the bookstore around us. "Isn't that what we're trying to do here? I mean, the only thing stopping them from becoming Potters themselves is seeing the example of something better. That's why I showed them the movie, and that's why I brought it into the game. These kids aren't into fantasy. Oh, they have fun on Saturdays, but then they go out into their real world, and there's little that's noble out there for them."

"But if you can get them to see the nobility in themselves…"

"That's right. That's it exactly. But if I just have them pretend they're knights of some high mucky-muck fantasy order, the Sacred Knights of the White Star, for instance, it's fun for an hour or so but it doesn't take. It's just a game."

"But they can relate to someone like George Bailey. Calling them Knights of Bailey grounds it in the real world."

"That's the idea. At least, I hope it does."

I whistled. "Stanley, that's brilliant. You really get these kids, don't you?"

"Get them? Hell, Boss, I'm one of them! I was raised in a neighborhood just like this one. It was a Bailey that got me out, gave me a chance." He glanced at his watch. "Hey, look, I'd be happy to talk more about this, but, um…."

"You have a date."

51

He grinned. "Got it in one, Boss. I need to go. See you Monday?"

"See you Monday. And thanks for the explanation."

He shouldered his backpack and headed out the door. Mary sauntered over. "Hot date?" she asked, indicating the figure of Stanley disappearing into the lightly falling snow outside.

"So he says. How about you? Why don't you take off, too? It's about closing time anyway, and I can take care of any customers that might come in."

"Why, thanks, John. I think I will. I have some shopping still to do."

"Well, go do it, then. I'll see you on Monday."

She smiled. "OK, but don't give the store away before then."

I placed my hand on my chest. "Cross my heart!"

After Mary left, I puttered about the bookstore, straightening books on shelves, adjusting some of the displays, all the while thinking about what had happened that afternoon. Outside the snow had stopped falling, and for a short time at least, everything was covered in a pristine whiteness. It wouldn't last, I knew. Whatever else the city did, it could turn snow into dirty slush with amazing efficiency and speed.

Finally, I locked the front door and turned the OPEN sign to CLOSED. I sat down in one of the easy chairs placed here and there around the store, creating little nooks where kids could sit and read books. *Powers visited here today*, I thought wonderingly. I cast my inner sensitivities out into the bookstore, but I couldn't feel anything out of the ordinary.

It had been years since I'd last been in a magical lodge or taken part in any kind of ceremony. The group into which I'd been initiated had long since disbanded after the death of the man who'd been its founder. He'd been a spiritual mentor to me—to all of us, really, who'd been part of his circle—and with his passing, there'd been no one to replace him. His wife, a highly skilled mage in her own right, tried for a time, but we could see her heart wasn't in it. So we all went our separate ways.

For me, my path took me into business, and I discovered I had a knack for it. Whatever I touched seemed to flourish, and one success followed another. But at the peak of my career, I remembered something my mentor had said. We were driving through the seedier parts of the city, not far, actually, from where I was now sitting. He'd pointed out the window to a group of kids standing on a street corner. "There's the future," he said. "The old magical lodge system is over. The time of teachers like me is past. A new kind of spiritual center needs to come into being, something anchored in the world these kids know so they can relate to it." He didn't say anymore, but his words stayed with me for years.

Sitting in my plush corporate office one day, I felt the time had come to try to start just such a center in the city, a place where the Powers of Spirit could be focused to reach out and help the youth who were the future and who might otherwise be lost. Not that I felt I was a spiritual teacher, certainly not of the caliber of my own mentor. But I knew I had some skills, and in my fifties, I knew it was time to put them to use in service to something other than making money.

I chose to start a bookstore because I love books, and I wanted to share that love with others. Because I didn't need to make more money, I could afford to run it at a loss, giving books away when it was appropriate, offering other services like the game days and the movie nights, providing meals, and so on. As Mary had said, it was a kind of social service center but for me, in my heart of hearts, it was an attempt to create a spiritual center of the kind my mentor had said was needed.

Frankly, I'd not been sure I was anywhere close to succeeding. But today, the Powers had visited, taking over a silly fantasy game and turning it into something very much more. Why They had done so, I had no idea. Only time would reveal Their reasons. But tonight I took it as an affirmation that I was succeeding in my basic intent. A spiritual center, a new kind of ashram, *was* coming into being, after all, however modest the scale. I felt immensely grateful.

At that point, I must have drifted off to sleep, for I found myself standing in front of the egg-shaped altar that Stanley had described, one I had often seen before in dreams. Above it, the silver flame burned with a steady Light. The area around me was lost in a mist that reflected the Light back, so I was enfolded in a soft illumination. Suddenly, the flame pulsed and a thin stream of Light reached out and touched me. I felt a flare of energy. The mists disappeared. I was floating high in the sky above the city. It was gleaming like a collection of fiery jewels, but the radiance was broken up here and there with patches of greyness where the Light struggled to shine through. In one of these patches, a thin column of Light shot upwards, and I realized I was seeing my bookstore as it looked from the astral realm.

I felt a moment of awe that anything I had created could have brought that shining ray of Light into being. But as I watched, a blot of darkness moved into the surrounding patch of greyness, oozing towards this thin column of Light. Alarm shot through me.

My heart beating against my chest, I found myself back in the bookstore, sitting in the chair where I had obviously dozed off. In front of me stood a figure clothed in Light. I was astonished to see that it looked just like Jimmy Stewart, the actor. He pointed a finger at me. "Potter comes," he said in his distinctive drawl.

"What?" I said, confused.

"Potter comes!" And then he faded away.

From a distance, I heard a pounding. It grew louder, and with a jerk, I finally completely woke up. I realized I'd still been dreaming when I'd seen the Stewart figure.

The pounding continued. Someone was at the front door. Groggily, I got to my feet and went to the door, shouting, "We're closed!"

From outside, I heard Eddie the cop's voice, loud and urgent.

"John, open up! Open up!"

I got to the door and unlocked it, opening it. Standing just outside, Eddie's face was screwed up in concern and alarm. "Eddie!" I exclaimed. "What's the matter?" In the distance, I could hear a cacophony of sirens filling the air.

He gripped my arm. "John, close your shutters. There's a riot headed this way!"

"What?" I said in confusion. My brain still wasn't fully engaged.

"John, your shop is in danger. The whole street is."

"What's happened?" Eddie's urgent concern was finally getting through to me.

He sighed. "There was domestic disturbance. Two cops went to help, but it turned nasty. One cop was injured, and his partner shot the husband. Killed him."

"Omigod!"

"That was thirty minutes ago. The news went out immediately on social media, and a flash mob appeared out of nowhere. Now a riot's broken out, and its headed down the street this way. People are smashing and burning stores as they go."

Even as he spoke, I could smell the smoke in the air and something else. Tear gas.

"We mobilizing, but the crowd is building faster than we can contain it. It's almost like something alive, and it's headed this way. I'm warning all the shop owners along here. You, John, need to get your shutters down." All the store fronts along the street had metal barriers that could be lowered over the windows to prevent break-ins. I just hadn't bothered to lower mine yet.

"OK, Eddie, thanks for the warning!"

"Gotta go, John. Good luck! I'll be back as soon as I can."

"Take care, Eddie," I said, and sent him a silent blessing as he headed off down the street to warn others.

I immediately lowered the shutters that protected the

windows. The sirens were growing louder and closer, and the smell of smoke was becoming more pungent. I could also now hear the yelling and chants of a mob. I flashed on the image of the dark blot I'd seen invading the patch of greyness around the bookstore and of Jimmy Stewart standing in my bookstore, pointing at me and saying, "Potter comes!"

Potter, indeed! Some force was actively seeking to destroy the small center of Light I was trying to create, to take away any chance that the kids of this neighborhood might rise beyond the helplessness and hopelessness around them.

But why now?

I knew in an instant it was because the Powers had come today, blessing the kids and setting something into motion. *When Light acts, Darkness reacts*, my mentor had said once. Tonight, it seemed like he'd been right.

The window shutters down, I thought for a moment of retreating into the bookstore before the mob arrived. But I knew I couldn't do that. Whatever was coming, I was going to face it.

I stood outside the bookstore and waited. I could see people running down the street, shrouded in smoke, and could hear the cries and shouts as the mob came closer. In the distance, a car burst into flames. I opened my inner sight. Hovering above the street in the distance was a miasmic cloud shot through with streaks of reddish light. *Anger*, I thought. *Hatred*. Mindless energies seeking only to destroy, a parasite feeding on the emotions of the humans within its sway. And at the center of this cloud, I could see a figure, a concentration of will and malevolence. It looked just like a bloated Lionel Barrymore, the actor who had portrayed Henry Potter in the movie.

The Potter!

Whatever or whoever it was in reality, it was an agent of darkness presenting itself to my imagination as an image from *It's a Wonderful Life*, fully intent on making life in this city anything but.

It had been years since I had really worked as an operative mage, dealing with subtle energies good and bad, whole and broken. But like riding a bicycle, some skills you don't forget even if you don't practice them regularly. Reaching deep into the core of Light within me, I drew on my training and prepared myself for the encounter I knew was coming. Whether I would survive it was another matter, but I knew I couldn't give in to any fear now or all would be lost.

The cloud of dark subtle energies and the crowd of angry rioters within it, acting mindly under its influence, came ever closer. More cars burst into flame. Streetlights went dark as they were smashed by the mob. And did I hear gunshots? I wasn't sure.

Sirens said police were on their way, but would they arrive in time in sufficient numbers? Everything was escalating very fast. As cell phones multiplied the news throughout the city, more and more people, drawn by their own resentments, angers and frustrations, arrived to feed the cloud and surrender to its influence.

I knew what I needed to do. A direct assault on the Potter-figure at the heart of the cloud would disperse it, I hoped, causing the cloud to lose some of its energy. It wouldn't happen quickly, though. I needed time. The question was, would I have that time before the mob reached me? And even if I succeeded, would it be enough? A momentum was building that had nothing to do with the influence of subtle forces. Pent up angers were being released from hearts long burdened and denied.

I began to gather the energies of Light within myself, but at that moment, it seemed my time had run out. A group of hooded figures emerged out of the darkness running towards me, and I braced myself for the confrontation that I knew was imminent. As they got nearer, though, I saw with surprise and relief that it was Stanley and the kids from the role playing group, along with some of their friends.

"Stanley! What are you doing here?"

"Protecting the bookstore, I hope," he said. He turned to the boys and girls around him. "All right," he shouted. "Knights! Link up!" At that, about twenty kids joined arms and formed a cordon along the street in front of the bookstore.

"Stanley," I protested. "These are kids. Get them out of here. They could be hurt or killed."

"No can do, Boss," he said. "This was their idea. They were on their way here when Clarence called me on my cell phone and told me what was going down. I figured if I couldn't stop them, I'd join them." He grinned. "Guess that initiation took, eh?"

"You're all a bunch of bloody fools, and I wish you'd get them out of here!" I realized, though, that these kids could be stubborn as hell and not unfamiliar with danger in their lives. If I wanted a band of warriors at my side, I probably couldn't pick better ones. I knew, too, that many in the approaching mob would be from the neighborhood and would know these kids. They would think twice before doing something that might harm their own children or the children of their friends.

And, whether I approved or not, it could give me the time I needed to challenge the Potter-thing.

I pressed my back against the door of the bookstore. Drawing on the Light within me and from within the energy field of the bookstore, I found an intensity of power I didn't remember ever feeling before. I realized that that the burst of Light from the flame above the altar in my dream or vision had done something to me. My own initiation, perhaps? Whatever the reason, I was grateful.

I drew the Light out and formed it in my mind into a laser-like ray which I sent directly into the approach cloud of darkness, straight towards the Potter figure. The thing about Light is that it doesn't really fight darkness. It doesn't need to. Where Light is, darkness cannot be. My task was simply to hold that beam of Light in the presence of the dark entity so that it could illuminate the local subtle environment. At that point, the entity would have to disperse like shadows in sunlight.

As the beam of Light hit the Potter figure, it began to writhe and lose its form. But it was stronger than I'd hoped. It held on, drawing energy to itself from the emotions of the mob, trying to bolster its existence. But the Light I was focusing was strong, and I could feel Powers joining me, adding Their strength.

I could feel the entity growing desperate. As I watched, a dart of darkness shot out in our direction, but it disappeared before it did anything, at least as far as I could tell. Whatever it had been, it had had no effect. Or so I thought.

At that moment, the door to Abernathy's dry cleaning store flew open, and old Abernathy himself came stumbling out. I realized seeing him what I hadn't really noticed before. He did resemble the Potter figure from the movie. I also realized something else. He was surrounded by the dark aura projected by the entity. And he was carrying a shotgun, and he had it pointed right at Clarence who was holding the protective cordon closest to Abernathy's store.

"You mothereffer," he snarled. "I'm going to blow you away!"

"No!" I shouted. In that moment, I felt a flare of Light shoot out from me to him. The dark aura around him quivered and shrunk, but did not entirely disappear. Abernathy, however, stepped back, momentarily confused. I ran forward, putting myself between him and Clarence. "Abernathy, don't be a fool. These kids are here to protect us."

As I said this, Clarence, realizing what I was saying, pulled the line in our direction, extending it further down the street so that it would be between the fast approaching mob and the dry cleaners as well. Seeing the kids move, Abernathy trembled with rage. "Stop, or I'll shoot!"

I reached out and pulled the shotgun in my direction, pressing it against my chest. "You'll have to kill me first, Abernathy. Are you willing to do that?" Again, I felt Light flaring out from me and flowing around him. Suddenly, the dark aura around him dissipated and disappeared.

"What?" he stammered, confused.

"It's all right, Abernathy," I said, pulling the shotgun out of his hands and passing it to Stanley who had appeared by my side, ready, I was sure, to knock the old man out if he had to. "It's all right. These kids are here to protect us and our stores."

"Protect us?" I could see him struggling to grasp the concept.

"Yes. But it's still dangerous out here. Go back inside. The police are on their way."

Obediently, he turned and went back inside. I'd never seen Abernathy so meek, but I wasn't going to look a gift horse in its mouth.

"Good Jedi mind trick, Boss," Stanley said beside me. "Well done."

I chuckled. "We'll see." I turned my attention and my energy back towards the Potter-thing, but to my relief, I found it almost gone. It had shot its bolt trying to control Abernathy, and when it failed, it succumbed to the Light that was surrounding it.

However, we still had the mob to deal with, and by now it had reached us: men and women with stones, clubs, torches, whatever they could put their hands on with which to do damage to a world they felt had damaged them. But when they saw the cordon of kids, they stopped.

I stepped up to the cordon, and two young men dropped their hands long enough for me to step through. I wasn't about to hide behind youngsters. "These are your children," I shouted to the men at the front of the throng. "Are you going to hurt them?"

A voice rang out from the mob. "Clarence, go home!"

Clarence yelled back. "No! We're not going to let you hurt anyone here. *You* go home."

There was some more cursing and shouting, but no one made

a move. Around us, I could feel the cloud of negative energies beginning to disperse without the power of the Potter-entity to hold it together. It gave me hope we were going to make it through this.

"We may not like it, but the street is our home, too, and this bookstore is a place that's good to us," Clarence called out. "We won't let you harm it, or anything else."

More muttering from the crowd, but I could see bricks being dripped and clubs lowered. "Go home," I said again. From behind me, all the kids yelled out, "Go home!"

And they did. Like the cloud of dark energies that had driven them, the mob itself began to disperse, individuals coming to their senses and walking away.

Of course, it was at this point that Eddie and his reinforcements from the police department arrived, taking charge and moving everyone along. And it began to snow again. The danger was over.

Stanley, Clarence and the rest of the boys and girls—I should really say young men and women—clustered around, talking excitedly about what they'd done. I shook Clarence's hand and said, "Thank you for what you did, what you all did. You really were knights tonight."

"Knights of Bailey!" he said, grinning. "Just like you, man!"

Later that night, Stanley and I sat in two of the comfortable chairs in the bookstore and sipped mugs of hot cocoa.

"Whew, Boss. That was close. I wasn't sure we were going to get through it. And when old Abernathy appeared with that shotgun. Man, talk about scary!"

"I don't think we'll have as much problem with him, Stanley. He changed, too. It was the kids. They made the difference, and you, my man, made the difference for them. You made them knights."

"They made themselves knights, John. That kind of

knighthood is in us all. But the world is still going to be tough for them. Lots of Potters out there, lots of Pottersvilles."

"Yes. But we'll transform them all eventually. I have hope. Fiery hope!"

And I did. These weren't just words I used to comfort myself in the face of an angry, often mean-spirited world. I now knew them to be true.

Why? Well, it's simple.

I'm a Bailey and Baileys change the world.

CAPTAIN CHRISTMAS

Joe Powdoski loved Christmas. He loved everything about it: the decorations, the lights, the Christmas trees, the holly, the mistletoe. He loved the good cheer, the way people were more kindly to each other than at other times of the year. He loved eggnog and even fruit cakes. But most of all, he loved Santa Claus.

More precisely, he loved being Santa Claus.

Of course, he wasn't the real Santa. He was what parents always refer to as a "Santa's Helper," a stand-in for the real Man in Red who only shows up on Christmas Eve night. But though Joe didn't live at the North Pole with reindeer and elves and had no magical powers, he was about as close to the real thing as you could find. He had a fine, fluffy white beard and a full head of equally white hair. Even his eyebrows were bushy and white. His cheeks were rosy, and his eyes twinkled. He had a deep, rollicking belly laugh that turned his "Ho, Ho, Ho" into an irresistible contagion of laughter for all who heard it. And speaking of bellies, he was just round enough in all the right places to have the snuggliest lap for children to sit on.

Did I say he had no magical powers? Actually, when you were in Joe's presence, whether he was wearing a Santa suit or not, you couldn't help but feel happier and filled with goodwill. The spirit of Christmas just seemed to always be there around him, like fragrance around a flower. What could be more magical than that?

It had been over forty years since Joe had first put on a red suit at Christmas. At the time he had been a young man serving in the Peace Corps in Costa Rica. Some of the villages where he worked were very poor, and the children had little in the way of toys and treats. So he had hired a donkey, filled saddle bags with candy and little toys, dressed up in a red suit and fake beard, and had ridden through the villages, giving out his treasures to the children who ran delightedly alongside him, pleasing everyone except the local policeman who was afraid he would incite a riot.

After that, he was hooked. When he returned to America, he had immediately applied to be a Santa's Helper. For the first few years, he just stood on street corners ringing a bell to encourage people to put money in a small pot that hung on a stand beside him. Sometimes, when it was raining or snowing, he would end up looking as bedraggled as a red-furred mouse that had just climbed out of a river. But whatever the climate, he never lost his good cheer.

Of course in the beginning he had to wear a fake beard and makeup and he would stuff a pillow under his suit to make himself look fat. But as he got older, he grew a beard of his own which he could dye white. Then the time came when he no longer had to use any dye, and certainly no longer had no need for any pillows. During that time he graduated from being a street corner Santa to being a department store Santa, whose lap became the temporary home to the acquisitiveness and dreams of thousands of children. Then he began to train other people to be Santa's Helpers. Eventually, as the city's best-known and best-loved Santa, he would be invited to host special events and to attend children's parties. Every doctor in every hospital where there were children would swear that their young patients healed twice as fast after a visit from Santa Joe. He especially loved delivering presents to needy children, and no one really knew how many secret trips he made with special gifts he got himself so that as far as possible no family and no child in his city would go without on Christmas morning.

Even with all these visits and parties and appearances filling up his schedule during the Holidays, when there was a need—or even when he just felt like it—he would still go out and stand on a street corner to ring a bell just for old times sake and to watch the faces of passersby light up when he laughed his "Ho! Ho! Ho!" and wished them a Merry Christmas.

Which is what he was doing on a cold, clear night three days before Christmas. It was late, and most shoppers had gone home to their warm houses and apartments. Only the most dedicated—or greedy—of merchants still had their stores open to serve the most persistent—or desperate—of shoppers. Yet Joe, dressed in his full Santa regalia, stood on the corner in a pool of light shed by a lone streetlamp, still ringing his bell, a figure of cheer and goodwill for those remaining few abroad on the streets before the city finally went to sleep.

Suddenly, there was a whooshing sound from above him and a sense of something falling from the sky. He looked up just in time to see two figures descend like angels out of the night sky, landing lightly on the sidewalk before him.

One was a man, but to say that is like saying that Russell Wilson and Tom Brady are only quarterbacks or that Chris Hemsworth was just an actor. He was about six and a half-feet tall, well-built, dressed in a tight-fitting red suit trimmed with white around the color and cuffs, with black boots and black belt. Around him a white cape with red trim billowed in the cold night breeze.

Did I say he was well-built? Buff is the word. His body was strongly muscled yet perfectly proportioned, suggesting unlimited strength coupled with supple grace. His head was bare, his hair a blond so light as to be almost white, and his face was more than movie-star handsome. He was young-god handsome. And he seemed to shimmer with vitality in the dark.

The other was a woman, but saying that is like saying Helen of Troy was just another pretty face or Marilyn Monroe just an actress. She was only a little shorter than her companion, and she was dressed in a skin-tight costume made of vines and leaves, holly and ivy. To say this may make it sound like she was dressed like a bush, but the effect only emphasized her obvious femininity, making her heart-stoppingly beautiful. Even Joe, who had been happily married for almost as many years as he had been wearing a Santa Claus suit, found his pulse quickening to look at her and his cheeks got even redder than usual. Instead of a cape like her companion, she had lustrous long hair that shone a reddish gold in the streetlight and that fell in glorious waves almost to the calves of her legs. If the man was like a god made flesh, then she was all that any goddess would ever hope to be.

To say that Joe was surprised by his visitors would be putting it mildly. His eyes goggled. His hand stopped ringing the bell. His mouth fell open. Even his red furred cap suddenly slipped askew on his head. Instead of his hearty "Ho! Ho! Ho!" or a cheery "Merry Christmas," all he could say was, "Well, I'll be........"

The man stepped forward, smiling an impossibly perfect smile that positively shone in the night. "Have we the pleasure of speaking to the famous Santa Claus?" he asked, his voice as deep as a canyon and as cultured as pearls.

"Well, yes....that is....uh..." was all poor Joe could stammer out.

"Fine! Fine! It is a privilege to meet you!" The man took Joe's limp, gloved hand and shook it, and Joe felt the indescribable power of the man's touch, as if the mightiest mountain on earth had suddenly bent down and taken hold of his hand. "I am Captain Christmas and this is my partner." He turned and extended his hand to the woman who took it gracefully and stepped forward. "Lady Mistletoe."

"A pleasure, dear man," she said, and she leaned forward and kissed Joe on the forehead. An electric shock passed through him. His bell fell from his nerveless fingers. In that moment, all the good cheer he normally felt throughout the year seemed like the palest imitation of the real thing as he experienced a giddy merriment beyond anything he had imagined. He giggled as she pulled away, and nearly lost his balance.

She smiled at him, and her smile was, if anything, even more dazzling than that of her companion. "We were flying overhead to the North Pole to visit you when with our super hearing we heard your laughter coming from this city. We were astonished to see you alone on this street corner ringing a bell, but we knew right away it was you, so we flew down."

"Yes," the man added. "It is lucky for us indeed, having just arrived on your world, to have found you so soon. There is much to do, and we wish to get started as soon as possible."

"Do? Get started...?" Joe's mind had not yet slipped back into gear.

"Why, yes, Santa Claus. We are your replacements, Captain Christmas and Lady Mistletoe. We have come to take over Christmas for you."

"Take over Christmas...?" The words still did not make sense.

Lady Mistletoe glanced at her partner, then looked back at Joe. He realized that her eyes were a deep forest green, and they seemed to beckon him into mysterious depths he could only guess at. Then he closed his eyes and shook his head to clear it. What were these strangers trying to tell him?

"I realize this must come as a shock to you, though a pleasant one, I hope," said Lady Mistletoe, her voice like rich, smoky honey. "You must have resigned yourself to many more centuries of having to ride around in that antiquated sleigh pulled by flying quadrupeds. Just because that is what mortals expect. I can only imagine your despair. It must have seemed like a prison sentence..."

"Which is why we have come, my good man...or elf," Captain Christmas continued. "As is appropriate at this time of year, we say to you, 'Rejoice, for we bring you tidings of good cheer!' Your job is over, Santa Claus. Finally, after all these centuries, you can now retire!"

"Yes," said the woman, brightly. "You can retire!"

Joe Powdoski had no idea who these people were, no idea how they had flown down from the sky, or where they had come from. But through the haze of his astonishment and, he had to admit, the kiss-induced confusion, one thing suddenly stood out very clearly. These refugees from a superhero comic book were telling him he should retire and not be Santa Claus anymore!

And with that, Joe☉s fighting instincts were aroused, his passion was challenged, and his mind became as clear as a wintry Christmas Eve. He spoke, his words turned eloquent by his indignation. ☉Retire? Hey, no way, José!☉

He glared at the two glorious beings before him, a Yule fire blazing in his eyes. "I'm just reaching my prime as Santa Claus. So go back where you came from, wherever that is and whoever you are!" He reached down to pick up his bell from the pavement.

Captain Christmas and Lady Mistletoe looked at each. "Oh dear," she said, "I didn't think he would be stubborn."

"It's all right, Lady Mistletoe" Captain Christmas assured her. "It's really my fault. I shouldn't have blurted it out without some buildup." He turned back to Joe. "I'm sorry, Santa. I should have explained more before just 'laying it on you,' as the mortals say. Let's see. Where should I begin?"

"You can begin by flying back wherever you came from," Joe said. Both his grandfather and his father had been prize fighters in their youth, and though Joe had never struck anyone himself, he could feel the ancestral feistiness rising within him. He had to protect what was most dear to him.

"Now, now," said Captain Christmas. "Hear us out, and you will see reason is on our side. Look." The red and black garbed man suddenly rose into the air so that Joe was eye level with the tips of his shiny black boots. After a moment, the woman rose up next to him. "As you can see, we can fly. Can you? That is, without your sleigh?"

"Well," Joe said, "no, I can't, but then, I'm not San...."

"Well, we can," Captain Christmas said, interrupting him, "and it would be a great advantage in our work. Furthermore....."

There was a sudden whoosh, and Joe almost fell on his face as the suction of a wind pulled him forward. His Santa's cap, however, did go sailing up into the air and down the street. Then, there was another whoosh, and this time the wind nearly knocked him backwards. Captain Christmas was floating in the air above him once more, holding both his cap and a brilliant flower that looked tropical in origin and which was dripping with water. "..... We can fly very fast! Here is your cap, Santa, and here, my dear, is a flower from the Amazonian rain forest." He handed the plant to Lady Mistletoe, who bowed gracefully to him.

"So you see, we would have no need of your flying animals or that old sleigh," said Lady Mistletoe. "We are also very strong. You have seen how a growing plant can crack pavement?" She landed on the street near Joe and plunged the finger of one hand into the asphalt as if it were nothing harder than a Christmas pudding. With hardly any effort, she ripped up a large segment of pavement and waved it about in the air with one hand while bringing her flower up to her nose with the other. "Ah, it smells divine, Captain Christmas!" Then she tossed the chunk of asphalt to him. He caught it, flew over the road and dropped it back into the hole it had left in the street. A blaze of light erupted from his eyes, playing over the pavement like laser beams. Before Joe could blink, the street was whole again.

Captain Christmas looked back at him with a grin. "We have other powers as well, such as the ability to manipulate matter just with the power of our gaze!"

Joe whistled in amazement.

"But this is not really relevant to Christmas," the man said, landing once more in front of Joe. "Christmas is about giving, and bringing toys to children everywhere."

"It's about more than just that," Joe interrupted.

"Oh yes, it's also about bringing good cheer and merriment," said Lady Mistletoe. "Well, that's my department, and I assure you, I am well endowed with the powers for that task." She paused as if expecting Santa to protest, but on this point, Joe had no argument. She shrugged. "Observe," and she waved her hand.

Suddenly the front of the building next to them was festooned with greenery and lights. Even the bricks seemed to fairly ooze good cheer and cozy fellowship. Once again, Joe began to feel light-hearted and giddy, as if he had had a few too many glasses of Christmas punch. He shook his head and stomped his feet to bring back the fighting spirit of his father and grandfather.

"Yes, yes, dear, all that is quite important, I'm sure," said Captain Christmas, "but the real thing is the giving. It's delivering toys under the trees. And we can do that far more efficiently than you."

He opened his hand, and a small metal disk materialized in his palm. It was colored red with the letters "C C" emblazoned in gold upon it. "This is a Captain Christmas Christmas Disk. You put it under the Christmas Tree on Christmas Eve like this...."

Halfway down the block was a potted tree around which the city had draped colored tinsel. Captain Christmas flew down to it and put the disk on the pavement by the cement pot. He flew back to stand next to Santa Joe.

"Then precisely at 2:34 am in the morning, when everyone is sure to be asleep, I press a button on my orbiting space station..."

"Which is invisible," added Lady Mistletoe. "Advanced stealth technology and all that..."

"Yes, and, as I was saying, I press the button and faster than you can say Merry Christmas..." Captain Christmas mimed pressing a button on his palm. There was a flash of light under the tree, and a pile of brightly wrapped presents appeared from nowhere. "All the presents arrive."

"No more climbing down smelly, dirty old chimneys," Lady Mistletoe said brightly. "And besides, most children these days don't live in houses with chimneys. Say, how do you get in to leave the presents anyway?"

"Uh...I'd...uh...rather not say," stammered Joe, who had no idea how Santa did it and wouldn't have told these two even if he did know.

"That's all right, old man," Captain Christmas said heartily. "I understand you have your trade secrets, not that it matters anymore. But I reveal all my methods so you can retire with confidence. You see, we use simultaneous matter transmission from our secret city on the far side of the moon, the side that you can never see from the earth."

"And the best part," Lady Mistletoe said, "is that every child will get exactly what he or she wants."

"But...how...how will you know what they want?"

The two laughed. "Why, through our website, of course: *CapChris.com*. All a child has to do is send us his or her wish list and we make the toys in our moon base," explained Captain Christmas.

"Much more modern and believable than the North Pole. Why did you ever pick such a cold, barren place anyway?" Lady Mistletoe asked.

"Like the far side of the moon is warm and lush?" Joe said sarcastically.

"No, of course not," said Captain Christmas. "The point is that it's inaccessible and therefore has mystery. At one time the North Pole must have held mystery, too, because no one could get to it. But now thousands of people fly over it every day. It's become, well, pardon me for saying it, but...ordinary."

As far as Joe was concerned, the North Pole was still as mysterious as ever, but he let that pass. Something Captain Christmas had said earlier had caught his attention instead. "What did you mean when you said you made the toys in your moon base?"

"Why, just that. Whatever the child wants, we can make it with our robots and matter manipulation chambers. Just think, no more Christmas stress trying to shop or wondering how to afford the presents! Just let us know what you want, and we'll give it to you!"

"But...how will people pay you...?

"Pay?" said Captain Christmas. "There is no need to pay. Christmas is about giving, and we'll do the giving!"

"Furthermore, no child has to worry that he or she won't get whatever he or she asked for." Lady Mistletoe's eyes sparkled. "There won't be any surprises. Each child can sleep sure in the knowledge that what he or she wanted will be under the tree." She laughed, and for the first time, Joe truly felt a thrill of fear in the presence of these two superbeings.

"But," he said, "that would destroy Christmas! What would Christmas be without the anticipation of Christmas morning, wondering whether your wishes would be granted; yes, even the worry. If you take away surprises, you take away Christmas."

"No, no. If you bring certainty into the process, you take away stress. You increase good cheer and merriment!"

"And no shopping?" Joe went on as if Lady Mistletoe hadn't spoken. "Why, part of the fun of Christmas is shopping. Oh, I know it goes to extremes, and everything gets too commercialized. But there is pleasure in trying to find just the right gift or in thinking about what a person might really want or need, or in anticipating their pleasure when they open a package and it's something totally unexpected that only you could have thought of or made for them. And what about the store keepers? Many of them make most of their money in Christmas sales. If no one needs to buy any Christmas presents, well, I know it sounds wonderful, but... the whole economy could collapse."

"Why, Santa Claus, are you defending greed and people going into debt at what should be the happiest, merriest time of the year?" Lady Mistletoe looked skeptical.

"No, no..." Joe was getting confused. "No one likes that, it's not part of Christmas, but yet...yet....the way things are...."

"The way things are is old fashioned and due for a change!" Captain Christmas said firmly. "You have had nearly two thousand years to work your magic. And what is the result? Fewer and fewer people believe in you. Crass commercial interests hijack the spirit of Christmas for their own greedy ends. Children are disappointed on Christmas morning because they didn't get what they really wanted...or didn't get anything at all. Parents go into debt. More people are depressed than at any other time of the year. Can you really claim success? Don't you think it's time you retired and let younger people with newer ideas and abilities take over? Do you really want to see the current situation continue?"

"No....yes....no....I don't know!" Joe felt confused and overwhelmed. Yes, there were problems with Christmas, but it wasn't all bad. It wasn't all what they said, was it? Santa Claus retire? No more Santa Claus? Impossible! Yet, what did Santa have to offer that was better than what Captain Christmas and Lady Mistletoe could do? They made a good case, Joe had to admit!

But what was he doing even thinking about it? He couldn't make any decisions anyway. He wasn't Santa Claus, the ageless spirit of Christmas. He was only a Santa's Helper.

Then it struck Joe that if Santa Claus ever needed help, it was now. Or else these beings might really take over Christmas. Though he couldn't find the words to argue with them, he just knew in his heart that that would be a catastrophe!

So, come on, Santa's Helper, he thought. *Help!* But his brain was like mush. He couldn't think.

"So, Santa Claus, surely you see the rightness of our position. Surely you agree, you must step aside, step down, step away, and let us take over. Let the word go forth that from now on, Christmas is in the good hands of Captain Christmas..."

"And Lady Mistletoe!"

The two of them flew into the air, did some loop-the-loops, some barrel rolls, gave each other a high five fifty feet up, then swooped down to land in front of Joe again.

"Can we give you a lift to the North Pole, or do you have your flying quadrupeds hidden nearby?"

Then, in that very moment, as if a bit of magic entered into him, Joe knew exactly what to say and do.

"All right. You two make a very compelling argument, I must admit, and there is no doubt that you make a fantastic couple." The two magical superbeings smiled at each other. "But look, the choice is not mine to make."

Captain Christmas frowned. "What do you mean? Who else can make it?"

"Well, you see, I don't really work for myself. I work for children and their parents. They are the ones who must decide if they want me or you to represent them."

"But that is obvious! What child would not want to get whatever he or she wants on Christmas? And what parent would not want to stop the hassle of shopping and just have presents come for free?"

"That may be," and Joe felt an inner tremor that Captain Christmas might truly be right about this. What he was going to propose was certainly risky, but in that moment, he felt strangely confident that it was a good risk to take. "I challenge you to let a group of children and parents decide. Tomorrow I am scheduled to appear at a benefit for a local children's hospital. There will be many children and parents there. Let us put the case before them and let them choose. I promise if they choose the two of you, I will put away this suit and never wear it again. Christmas will be yours. But if they choose Santa, then the two of you must leave and not interfere. Do you agree?"

Lady Mistletoe laughed. "But of course we agree, you dear little man. I can see the need for such a formality, but the choice is already certain."

"Of course it is," said Captain Christmas. "But we will submit to your conditions."

"Good. Then meet me back here in the morning on this corner and you can fly me to the meeting. That way we will all arrive at the same time and it will be a fair contest."

"Very good. Then we will leave you now and fly back to

our fabulous city on the moon. But be ready, Santa Claus. After tomorrow, Christmas will be ours and you will be history!"

The next morning at the appointed time, Joe Powdoski, looking splendid in his red and white Santa suit with the black boots and black belt, stood on the street corner wishing passersby a Merry Christmas. Suddenly, there was a flash of red, white, and green, and he was gone. Several onlookers were blown over by the force of a sudden wind that whooshed down the street.

High above the city, Captain Christmas carried Santa Joe in his arms while Lady Mistletoe cruised along beside them, her long hair streaming like molten gold behind her, looking as alluring as ever. Clutching at his Santa hat with one hand lest it blow away, Joe used his other hand to point out a large building to his right. "That's the hospital over there. The meeting is in the dining room."

"Yes," said Captain Christmas, his eyes glowing with a strange energy. "I can see the people gathered awaiting you."

The two superbeings swooped down with their passenger, heading straight for the roof. For a moment, Joe thought they were going to smash into the building, for they showed no signs of slowing down or stopping, but at the last moment, a green beam shot out from a ring on Lady Mistletoe's hand, creating a tunnel of light right through the roof, through several ceilings and floors, and ending in the dining room at the lowest level. They shot through, appearing in the air above the startled gathering of children, parents, doctors, and nurses. There was a chorus of oohs and ahhs. Then the two landed, and Joe hopped down from Captain Christmas's arms.

"It's Santa Claus!" shouted the children. "Did you see how he came through the roof? Cool!"

Over in one corner, a dad turned to a doctor in a white coat and said, "Wow! Who's the babe with Santa?" At which point his wife, who had overheard, elbowed him sharply in the ribs. "Ow!"

he said, clutching his side in pain. The doctor, never taking his eyes off Lady Mistletoe, whispered in his ear, "I can fix that for you later in the emergency room..."

Up in front, Joe turned to his two companions and said, "Let me speak to them first." The superbeings nodded.

As soon as the commotion had settled down, Joe looked at the children and said, "Merry Christmas, my little friends."

"Merry Christmas," they all shouted back.

"This is not what I had planned to do today with you, but I have a special favor to ask you and your parents. It's a very important favor. Maybe the most important favor in the whole world. I need your help. Will you help me?"

"Yeeessssss!" shouted dozens of voices.

"Thank you! Then, without further ado, let me introduce to you two friends of mine who have come from....well, from somewhere a long way away. They have something to tell to you, and then you will have to make a choice. Making that choice is the favor I spoke about." He turned to point out his two companions. "I want you to welcome Captain Christmas and Lady Mistletoe!"

There was much shouting and stamping of feet and even a few whistles. Captain Christmas and Lady Mistletoe waved to the children and raised their arms above their heads in a victory clasp. Then they even flew around the room a few times, much to everyone's astonishment and delight.

Landing in front of the crowd, Lady Mistletoe waved her hands, and suddenly the whole room was filled with the scent of pine and holly, and there were vines and greens everywhere, all filled with sparkling lights. The whole room seemed like a fairy land. Even the children were hushed with wonder. Then the green-clad woman with the golden red hair blew a kiss to the whole gathering, and at least one half of the couples there erupted in spontaneous applause and shouting. The other half was conspicuously silent.

Finally, their bells and whistles finished, the two of them presented their case. They told about their secret base on the far side of the moon, never seen from earth, and about the robots and even a few aliens who helped them there. The children cheered, and Joe's heart sank a bit.

Then Captain Christmas showed them the matter transmitter disk and told them about always getting exactly what they wanted on Christmas morning, and the children cheered even more. Joe's heart sank even further.

He then told how he could make all the presents and no parent would ever have to spend money buying toys and gifts again. This time the parents cheered as well. Joe's heart plunged below the floor.

Finally, Lady Mistletoe came forward and, to Joe's surprise, said, "Through my powers and our superscience, I will visit every house on Christmas night and create a fully decorated tree. You will never have to get or decorate another Christmas tree again!" Once more there was wild cheering, though mostly from the dads, and Joe felt his heart land in the center of the earth.

"So, girls and boys, moms and dads," finished Captain Christmas, "we have come to give you all a truly Twenty-First century Christmas. No more reindeers landing and maybe pooping on your roof. No more worrying about Christmas morning and what's under the tree. No more standing in long shopping lines and paying big bills later. No more unbelievable North Pole hideaways and figuring out how Santa comes to places without chimneys. Just a happy, sure, scientific, predictable Christmas where we do all the work and you just reap the pleasures. That's what we bring you!" He rose into the air, did a tight backwards loop and landed like an acrobat, his hands in the air, a huge grin on his face. Somewhere in the back, a nurse swooned and fainted.

Everyone turned to look at Santa Joe. He could see the excitement in their eyes, the wonder, yes, even the greed at the thought of free presents...and he despaired. Why had he ever taken this foolish risk? Why had he ever issued this challenge? He could have told them he was only a Santa's Helper and let them go find the real Santa, who, Joe was sure, would have known exactly what to say and do. Of course he was going to lose. In his mind's eye, he could see himself hanging up his Santa suit, his career as Santa Claus—no, as a Santa's Helper—over. And some Helper he had turned out to be. He had just lost Christmas for Santa!

But then, amazingly, unexpectedly, he felt from somewhere deep inside a rich chuckle welling up, and before he could help himself, it burst forth in a loud, rich, rolling "Ho! Ho! Ho!" He laughed and laughed, and everyone in the room laughed with him, for when Santa Joe laughed, no one could keep a straight face.

Then a calm came over him. He got up. He wasn't sure what he was going to say, but he suddenly felt confident the words would be there.

He grinned at the children. "Children," he said, "and moms and dads, I said I had a favor to ask you. That favor is to decide who you want to represent the Christmas spirit from now on, Santa or Captain Christmas and the lovely Lady Mistletoe."

Somewhere in the back, a doctor, undoubtedly single, whistled and cheered, and Lady Mistletoe bowed gracefully.

"If you choose my friends," Joe went on, "then I will disappear, and you will never see Santa Claus again." Where did that come from, Joe wondered, even as the words left his lips. "And if you choose me, then Captain Christmas and Lady Mistletoe will leave." He grinned at them, and they grinned back, but they were the knowing, smug grins of people who already knew the outcome of a contest and can afford to be gracious.

"Before you choose, though, I have a couple of things to say, and I have some questions for you. In fact, let's do the questions first. This one is for the parents. Who would you rather have come into your house on Christmas Eve night, me or Lady Mistletoe?"

There was a pregnant silence, followed by some shuffling and embarrassed coughing from several of the men, but one glance at the women's faces told the story right away. One of the moms came forward and said, "No offense, Lady Mistletoe, but we'd rather have Santa. Besides, we like choosing our own Christmas trees and decorating them. Right, fellows?" and all the dads quickly nodded their heads.

"I see," said Joe, not daring to look at Lady Mistletoe behind him. "Then my next question is for the children. Whose lap would you rather sit on to tell what you want for Christmas, mine or Captain Christmas's?"

"Lap?" said Captain Christmas, surprised. "Who said anything about laps? You don't need a lap. We have a website!"

"But we like laps," said a little girl in the audience.

"Oh...I see...well, I suppose some of the old traditions aren't too bad...." Captain Christmas sat down on thin air. "All right, then, little girl. Come sit on my lap."

Shyly at first, the girl came forward, then tentatively sat on the lap of Captain Christmas. "Ow!" she said. "Your lap is hard! It's like sitting on a board or something!" She hopped off and ran over to Santa Joe, who had seated himself in a chair. With a gleeful laugh, she leaped onto his lap and buried her face into his beard. Then she turned to the audience and said, "Now, this is a lap!" Everyone laughed. She hopped down and ran back to her seat.

Disgusted, Captain Christmas floated to his feet. "Just remember the website," he said, "and always getting what you want."

"Oh, yes," said Joe. "That's a hard one to beat. You never know what Santa will bring. You tell him what you want, but it's not always there." Many of the children nodded, their faces creased with frowns. "I understand that it's disappointing. But sometimes there are reasons not to always get what you want. Learning to rise above disappointment is an important part of life. And besides, isn't part of the fun of Christmas not knowing? What fun is there in knowing exactly what's in the packages under the tree? You might as well just go down to a store and buy what you want. But you can do that any old day. That isn't Christmas, is it?" Several of the children shook their heads in agreement.

"And as for buying," Joe went on, "the promise of free presents must be very appealing to all the parents. I know better than anyone how many of you struggle to make ends meet and pay the bills. I know you can't always afford to get the gifts you would most like to give. And I know that Christmas is overly commercialized. It's not perfect. But we are the ones who can make it better, who have to make it better, for its imperfections are our imperfections. And think of this. If you choose Captain Christmas, then you won't be part of the gift-giving at all. It will be an impersonal thing. Order from a website and have it delivered. But where are you in that process? Where is your love? Where is your chance to be the giver? By taking Santa out of the picture, Captain Christmas takes the Santa out of you!"

He opened his arms wide. "Christmas doesn't belong to Santa. It shouldn't belong to them, either," he said, pointing at the two superbeings behind him. "Christmas belongs to you! It's your work, your effort, your sacrifices, your wondering, your surprises, your love that make it Christmas. And something greater as well, found in the very spirit we celebrate this time of year. It's not about superpowers and hidden bases on the moon or advanced science or letting someone else do all the work for you."

He looked at the children. "Yes, I know Santa Claus isn't as believable as he once was. But part of life is learning that sometimes the most true things in life can also be the most unbelievable. Like love. Or sharing with one another because you want to. Besides, Christmas isn't about believing in Santa, anyway. It's about believing in yourselves and in each other!"

He sat down again. "So, now it's up to you. If you choose me, then there will always be a Santa for you every Christmas, as long as you want him. And if you choose Captain Christmas and Lady Mistletoe, well, then....you will have them and all they have offered. What will it be?"

82

A silence fell upon the assembled children and parents, as well as the staff of the hospital. Then the little girl who had tried out the laps got up and came over to Santa Joe. Without a word, she climbed onto his lap and gave him a kiss on the cheek. One by one, then in twos and threes, the rest of the children followed until they were all clustered around him. Then the moms followed, and after them the dads. And when it was all over, the only two people in the room standing by a very crestfallen looking Captain Christmas and Lady Mistletoe were a doctor, who said to the two, "Would you mind meeting me in the lab later so I can run some tests on you?" and a little boy who tugged at Captain Christmas's cape and said, "Can you teach me to fly?"

Later, on the roof of the hospital, Santa Joe stood with the two superbeings. "No hard feelings?" he said.

"None," said Captain Christmas. "It wouldn't be in the Christmas spirit to have hard feelings, would it?" But as the man began to rise into the air, Joe could see he was disappointed. He could understand the feeling of wanting to be part of something so wonderful and magical as Christmas.

Lady Mistletoe came up and shook his hand. Then she kissed him again, but this time it felt just like an ordinary kiss from a good friend, filled with warmth but not superhuman. "You are an extraordinary person, Santa. In fact, you are the real Captain Christmas. I can see we still have much to learn from you."

Joe thought for a moment, then said, "You should know, I'm just an ordinary person. I'm not really Santa Claus."

Lady Mistletoe looked at him for a moment. "Are you sure?" she said. Then she rose into the air to join her companion on their way to the dark side of the moon...or wherever.

"We may be back, you know!" were Captain Christmas's parting words, shouted down as the two gained altitude and disappeared into the sky.

"Good," Joe shouted back. "Then you can be *my* helpers!'

The Green Man

David Spangler

THE GREEN MAN

I live alone, though I hope this will change when I propose to the Incomparable Sandy on Christmas Eve. We've been dating for nearly a year now. I think it's high time I popped the question. I suspect Sandy feels this way, too.

But Sandy is not the focus of this story, though she could be and probably should be. As far as my heart is concerned, she should be the center of every story.

I'm really in love.

Living alone, as I have done since leaving college ten years ago, isn't the center of my story, either. It's just a fact, an important fact so that you can appreciate how startled I was to discover, when I woke up that morning, a stranger in my kitchen. It was a matter of concern, a matter-for-calling-the-police concern, except...what do you do when the stranger has slightly pointed ears, green skin, and small horns sticking out of rumpled forest-green hair?

Are you really going to call the cops...or a psychiatrist?

I apologize. I'm getting ahead of my story. It begins with the fact that, even though I live alone, I decorate lavishly when it comes to Christmas. I love Christmas, almost as much as I love the Incomparable Sandy. And at the heart of it all, more than the lights, the candles, the decorations on the mantle, or the lawn ornaments that flash and twinkle in the dark, is the tree.

No artificial tree for me. Oh no. And none of those tree-farm, supermarket-parking-lot trees, either. It must be a real tree, a wild one, one that I have tromped through the forest to find, and one that I have cut down myself. Fortunately, the city where I live is surrounded by forests. Every year I try to go deeper and deeper into the wildwoods to find my perfect tree. The effort, the adventure, the challenge of getting the tree out of the woods, netted and tied to my snowmobile, and back to where my truck is...these are all part of the magic of Christmas. I mean, sweat goes into it, and cold feet, too, when the snow gets into my boots because I've stepped into a deep drift.

Not to mention having the hot chocolate, stirred with a peppermint stick, when I finally get the tree home and it's standing in my living room, a bit of real nature in an artificial world.

What's not to love?

I don't decorate the tree right away. I'm no monster! I give it a chance to acclimate itself to its new surroundings. I put water in its stand and then let it alone, allowing the pure, pine aroma to fill the house, allowing the branches to unfold from being secured with the netting I take with me to use in dragging it through the snow. I want to appreciate its naked beauty, unadorned by the human-made, ornamental accouterments of the season.

I let it stand, a visitor from another world, for two or three days before I begin to domesticate it, turning it into a display of human artistry. And I'm not one of those people who think they must cover every inch with lights and tinsel and hang two or three ornaments from every branch. Oh no! I strive to achieve a balance between the natural and the artificial. The tree is not just a canvas on which to display my decorative abilities. It is my partner, and I want its naturalness to shine through and complement those few lights and ornaments I place upon it.

My friend Tom says I'm just too lazy to really decorate the tree. What does he know? Year after year, he trots out an artificial tree he bought somewhere. Philistine! And displaying an electric Santa that wiggles its hips and sings "Jingle Bells" is not my idea of decorating one's apartment.

What does Sandy think? I don't know yet. I met her after the holidays last year and knew immediately she was the most beautiful woman I had ever seen. Incomparable, really. But I'm hoping she'll appreciate the effect I'm striving for: an ecology of lights and beauty crafted by human hands (well, more likely manufactured by machines, but one does the best one can as part of modern civilization), at the center of which is a representative of Nature, lightly adorned to form a subtle connection with its surroundings.

At any rate, that was my plan. Until I discovered the stranger in my kitchen.

It was the second morning after I'd brought the tree into my home. I planned to start decorating it that day, so it was with excitement that I awoke, rose from my bed, got dressed, stuck my phone in my pocket, and went into my kitchen for a hot mocha to get my own Christmas juices flowing. And there he was, his back to me, dressed in what looked like green rags, though where the cloth ended and his skin began was hard to tell.

"What the....who the hell are you and how did you get in here?" I have triple locks on my door, so it was a natural question. It's a nice enough neighborhood, but, well, you never know.

The figure turned to face me. I'm not sure what I expected to see, what with the ears and horns and all, but it was a perfectly normal human face. I would even say a beautiful one (though not, of course, as beautiful as the face of the Incomparable Sandy). Had he had fangs or a beard or some other trollish feature, I think I would have been less shocked than by the perfection of his features. Aside from horns, hair, ears, and skin color, he looked like a perfectly normal young man in his early twenties or even late teens. He could easily have been one of those male models you see cavorting with flimsily dressed young women while displaying some brand of jeans. Except, of course, for the, well, *otherworldly* features.

I'm sure I stood there like a fool, mouth agape, momentarily stunned into silence.

"Good morning, human," he said, his voice pleasant, though higher-pitched than I expected. What *had* I been expecting? That he would growl? He made a wide sweep with his arm, taking in the whole of the kitchen. "What is all this?"

"It's...it's a kitchen," I said. "Say, who...or what are you? How did you get in here?"

He smiled. It was a friendly enough smile until I noticed

that his teeth came to sharp points. "Why, you brought me here, human."

Now I knew I must be dreaming. I'd never had a lucid dream before, but I'm sure if I had done so, it would have felt just like this, with everything seeming perfectly solid and real. But it couldn't be real, because this was definitely no human being, and I equally knew, as surely as I knew I loved the Incomparable Sandy, that I had not brought this being into my home.

I shook my head. "I did not. You're a dream. Go away and let me wake up properly."

He laughed, and his eyes sparkled like emeralds. I don't mean this metaphorically. I mean there were little sparks of green light coming from his eyes. "You are awake, human, or at least, I think so. I confess I'm not sure what passes for being awake with your kind, but I can say without equivocation that you are not dreaming. I know because this," and he indicated my body with a vertical sweep of his hand, "is not a dream body."

Hearing this, I knew he must be real, because I never use words like "equivocation." So, he couldn't be a figment of my subconscious or even of my imagination. Could he? I leaned against the kitchen counter for support, for my legs suddenly felt weak.

"It's shock, I expect," the figure said. "You should sit down." He gestured, and one of the chairs next to the small kitchen table slid across the floor to me as if pushed by an unseen force. I did as he suggested. It was either that or fall on my face.

"I'm sorry to startle you like this," he went on. "But it's not my fault. You brought me here, and I'm naturally curious about where I find myself. You have the strangest things. You even have winter in a box." He pointed to the refrigerator.

"It's called a 'fridge,'" I said. I rubbed my forehead. I could feel a headache coming on. "I have no idea who you are or what you're talking about. I certainly don't remember bringing you home with me. That's not the kind of thing I would forget."

He looked thoughtfully at me while absentmindedly rubbing one of his horns. "I'll have to take your word for it. I have no idea what a human person can remember. Maybe you can only remember what happens between one sunrise and another. I, on the other hand, can remember the world before humans existed."

"I'll have you know my memory is perfectly fine. I can remember back to my childhood, and that's a good thirty…say, what did you say? Before humans existed?"

"Of course. My species is much older than yours."

"Your species." I rubbed my forehead again. The headache was getting worse. Forget the mocha. What a wanted now was good black coffee and a couple of Tylenol. Or maybe a shot of whiskey. "Just who or what is your species? And why, why, why are you here in my kitchen?"

My unwanted visitor eyed me speculatively. "I admit I don't know a lot about humans. Individually, that is. I've never conversed with one before, but then a human has never brought me into their house before. On the other hand, I know a great deal about humanity. After all, over the centuries, you have used us to feed your fires, to construct your homes, to build the ships that carry you across the oceans…."

"Wait a minute! Are you saying you're a tree?" Listening to him, a penny had dropped, though it must have been a higher-denominated coin, given how shattering it was to my world view. "That's insane! Trees don't show up in people's kitchens to talk with them!"

"Well, you're right. I'm not a tree. I would have thought even a human could see that! Does it look like I have branches? Roots? Surely you can see the difference."

I closed my eyes and shook my head. "All right," I replied, looking at my visitor. "I give up. What are you, then?"

"Why, I'm a tree spirit, of course." He gestured towards the living room on the other side of the kitchen door. "Of that tree in there. The one you brought into your home."

"A tree spirit." I made no attempt to hide the incredulity in my voice.

"Yes. A tree spirit. A Green Man. And since I'm going to be living with you, I wanted to know what my new home was like." He turned away and started examining the electric stove.

I sprung out of my chair, took two steps to reach my visitor, and grabbed his shoulders to spin him around, momentarily surprised that he felt solid and real beneath my fingers. Weren't spirits insubstantial? But then he wasn't there. Where he had been standing, there was nothing. My hands held only empty air.

"What the hell!" I exclaimed.

"Now, that was plain rude," his voice sounded behind me. I spun around to see the Green Man, as he called himself (and, I admit, with some reason), sitting in the chair I had just vacated, one rag-clothed leg casually draped over the other in a relaxed pose. "Do you always attack your roommates?"

"Roommates?" I shouted, wanting to spring at him again but realizing it probably wouldn't do any good. "What do you mean, 'roommates?' What did you mean about living together?"

He raised his eyebrows, which, of course, were green. "Oh my, I knew humans could be insensitive. It's a shared ancestral memory that all trees possess, you know, but I didn't realize they could be so dumb. Though," he pondered, putting a green finger against his green lips and looking thoughtful, "I should have expected it, what with climate change and all."

He pointed at me. "Listen while I explain it as simply as I can. You find tree. You cut down tree. You bring tree here. Tree is now in your home. Tree is my home. Now, my home is in your home, so your home is my home. *Su casa es mi casa.* Comprende? Is that clear enough?"

"You speak Spanish?" Where would a tree learn Spanish in an American forest? "And how do you know words like equivocation?"

"I speak all languages. Trees are in every country, listening to every language. Ancestral memory, remember?"

"I've got to be imagining this," I groaned. "This can't be happening."

"That's what I thought when your axe cut into my tree."

Now, my head was throbbing. "I really need some coffee and a painkiller. My head is killing me!"

"Stress, I would imagine," the Green Man opined. "And shock, like I said, suddenly having a new roommate. But what kind of roommate would I be if I couldn't help you out." He got up from the chair and walked over, raising his hand toward my head.

I flinched and jerked my head back. "What...what are you doing?"

"Hold still," he commanded, and he touched my forehead. I felt something, a tingling in my body, and suddenly my headache was gone.

"Wow!" I said. "My headache is gone!"

He gestured, and in his hand, a cup of steaming black coffee suddenly appeared. "You wanted this, I believe?"

"How...?"

"Oh, I saw it in your mind. You've been thinking about it quite strongly."

I took the coffee, relieved that there was a solid cup in my hand. "Yes, but how...."

"Magic," he said. "Oh, I could try to explain it, but I don't think you have the concepts to understand my explanation. I'm not even sure humanity has developed the right words yet. So, let's just call it magic."

I tried the coffee. It was hot, strong, smooth, and delicious. Frankly, I couldn't remember having a better-tasting cup of coffee. "Wow again," I said. "This is fantastic!"

"Thank you," he said. "And on my first try, too." I could see he tried not to look smug, but he failed.

Holding my cup gingerly, not entirely sure it might not

suddenly disappear, spilling burning coffee onto my hands, I made my way over to the second chair by the kitchen table. But if the cup disappeared, wouldn't the coffee disappear, also? It had been magicked up as well. My mind whirling with these thoughts, I sat down. The Green Man sat down in the other chair.

"Look," he said, "I know this is a lot to take in. It's a lot for me, too. Three days ago, I was content in a forest, surrounded by other trees, the earth beneath me, the sky above, birds nesting in my branches, ants crawling up my trunk, everybody happy. Why did you come into the forest for a tree anyway? Surely you could have found a tree closer to your home? Like at a supermarket, from a tree farm?"

"Who wants one of those? I wanted the adventure of going into the woods to find it. I wanted something from nature, a tree from the wilderness."

"Didn't you think that the wilder the forest, the more it might be protected by fairies?"

"Fairies? Really? No, of course not. Who believes in fairies?"

"You're asking *me*, a tree spirit? Fairies are my best friends. Never mind. I can see that wouldn't have stopped you. So now, I'm here, in a place with walls and a floor and a ceiling, a big, confined box surrounded by things I've never seen before. Like your 'fridge.' But am I freaking out? No! You've got to be resilient like me. Don't be stuck in your roots. Go with the flow, man!"

"You sound like a flower child."

"I suppose I am a flower child, though my tree doesn't have flowers."

I sighed. "I have no idea how to have a conversation with you. But I guess I'll have to learn if you're going to be staying here."

"Yep, right up to the day you get rid of my tree."

"Wait! Get rid of your tree? You mean, when I take your tree out, you'll go with it?

"Like I said. The tree is my home. Where it is, I am, at least until it dies."

"Then what? Do you die, too?" I hadn't thought about this, and the idea disturbed me.

"Who, me? Nah. I'm a spirit, remember. Immortal. When this tree dies, I'll find another to be my home. It's a pain, though. I liked this tree. I'd hoped it would grow to be two hundred feet high or more. Wow! What a penthouse view I'd have then!" He sighed. "I can cross off that ambition, at least for now." He looked around. "You know, when my tree dies, I don't *have* to find another tree. I could become a house spirit. After all, the walls here are made of wood. Close enough. Then I could stay here with you, permanently!"

I choked on my coffee. "No! Absolutely not. I live alone, at least until I marry the Incomparable Sandy. And I'd definitely not want a threesome in the house. Especially not with someone who looks like you!"

He preened. "Well, I do cut a handsome figure, if I do say so myself."

"Not what I meant," though I had to admit, he was pretty impressive, in a male model kind of way. "You've got horns. And green skin."

"What? You've got something against colored people? Say, are you a racist? I'd hate to have a racist for a roommate."

"Racist," I spluttered with indignity. "Absolutely not! Why, some of my best friends are…"

"Are what?" he interrupted. "Green? Blue? Purple? Chartreuse? Spirits come in all colors, you know."

"That's not what I meant! Stop putting words in my mouth. I meant, you're not a human color."

He waved aside my objections. "It doesn't matter, roomie. You're probably the only person who can see me anyway."

"You mean no one else can see you? Just me? How come

I'm so favored?"

"Well, you cut down the tree. It's karma, man."

I thought about this for a minute or so. "You mean, if Sandy comes over, she won't see you at all?"

"Not unless her third eye's open."

"Sandy does not have three eyes! She has a perfectly formed face, and a beautiful one, at that!" How dared this creature even think my Incomparable Sandy had three eyes? Of course, if she did, she'd still be incomparable, but in a very different way.

"I don't mean a physical eye. Chew a root, guy, don't you know anything? I meant that she was clairvoyant. You know, able to see into the subtle world."

I thought for a moment. "I don't think so. There's nothing subtle about her. Sandy has strong opinions, that girl, and she's not shy in sharing them."

It was the Green Man's turn to sigh and roll his eyes. "I can see communication is going to be a trial for both of us." He got up. "OK, enough talking. What are our plans for the day? What are we going to do?"

I got up, too. "Well, I had planned to decorate the tree…er, I mean your home."

"Great! That sounds like fun. I'd love to spruce up the old domicile, even if it is a fir." He chuckled and elbowed me as he passed by en route to the living room. "Spruce? Fir? Get it?" Then, seeing the look of dismay on my face, he shrugged and said, "Tree humor. You'll get used to it."

We went into the living room. Every surface held something: Santa Clauses, reindeer, snowmen, angels, candy canes, a creche, all the things one expects to find in a room decorated for Christmas. Normally, my long sofa occupied the space in front of the living room window. I had moved it to provide space for the tree that now stood in its place. In this way, once decorated and with lights, it could shine in the window for people outside to see. Next to the tree was a small box containing the special ornaments and the string of lights that I had planned to use. As I say, when it comes to tree decorating, I'm a minimalist.

"Hello, home," the Green Man said, seeing his tree. He turned to me. "So, what do we do now?"

I knelt by the box and began pulling out the items within it, spreading them onto the floor. "Now we put these all on the tree."

"You hang these from the branches."

"Well, yes." I hung a blue ornament on a branch to demonstrate. "See, they have these little hooks here."

"Yes, yes, I see," he said, picking an ornament up and examining it.

"But first, we should put up the string of lights. Though," I said, considering my experience in past Christmases, "we should first check to make sure they're working. I never know why, but Christmas lights tend to fail from one year to the next, no matter how carefully I put them away."

"Dark magic," he said, thoughtfully.

"I suppose…" I said, plugging in the string of lights to a wall socket. Happily, all the green, blue, red, and yellow bulbs came alive with light. "There!" I said. "Aren't they beautiful? They'll look great on the tree."

He looked at the pile of ornaments and the string of lights. "Is this it?"

"Well, yes. It may not look like much, but I don't want to cover up the beautiful naturalness of the tree. You see, there should be a synergy of…."

"If you didn't want to cover up the tree with lights and colorful gewgaws," he interrupted, "why didn't you leave it in the forest? It already looked natural and beautiful."

"That misses the point. Some decorations are needed to bring out…."

"Never mind. I'll take over from here." He made some

gestures in the air, and suddenly the tree was a pyramidal mass of light and color. No minimalism here! Ornaments hung from every branch, interwoven with ribbons and strings of twinkling lights, which, upon close examination, were more like miniature stars than the usual Christmas bulbs. If there were a tree under all the decorations, it was difficult to see.

I was speechless.

"There!" the Green Man said with evident satisfaction. "Now, that is what I call decorating." He smirked. "I wish the fairies could see this, what with all their talk about glamour and such. Oh, they always say our trees are beautiful in the forest, but I know they're secretly comparing them with the colorful realm they come from, and not favorably, either." He leaned close and whispered in my ear. "Fairies can be insufferably uppity. But don't let them know I said so. They can hold grudges. You never want to piss off a fairy!"

I stepped back. Frankly, looking at the tree hurt my eyes. I thought it better not to say so; I wasn't sure how safe it was to piss off a Green Man. "Well," I said, "that is...something. Certainly more than I had in mind."

"Isn't it? Pretty splendid, I'd say, especially for a first-timer. Say, there's no reason the fairies can't see this. You don't mind if I invite a few friends over?"

"Friends...?"

"Thanks! That's decent of you. Especially on our first day together, and all." He slapped me on the shoulder, making me stumble forward a step. "What friends?" I stammered.

"You'll love them!"

He began making complicated signs and gestures with his hands, and little popping sounds began echoing through the living room. Looking around, I saw small humanoid creatures...and some not so humanoid, or so small...materializing into existence, displacing the air around them. Some landed on the fireplace mantle, some on the sofa and chairs, some on the coffee table, but most on the floor. Some were the size of my finger, some as large as my hand, and some were two or three feet in height. They were garbed in colorful outfits, and some wore little red peaked hats. Some wore nothing at all but were covered in fur or scales or plain bare skin but with gossamer wings. Some were ugly and some were beautiful, with both extremes being breathtaking in their own way.

"Omigosh!" I breathed. As creatures kept popping into existence, I wondered how they were all going to fit, without spilling over into other rooms. Which, of course, they did. One fellow, shaped like a thin man made entirely of twigs even materialized on my head. "Sorry, gov'ner," he said, leaping off into the growing mass of exotica.

That's when the music started and the lights went down, except for the glow from the tree, and everyone started dancing. It reminded me of the one time I went to a rave at a local nightclub. Not my cup of tea, but here it was in my home. A fairy rave!

I felt two large hairy arms seize me around my waist, and I was lifted up from the floor as if I weighed less than a feather. Turning my head to see who had hold of me, I got a face full of fur. "Come, human," a deep, rumbling but friendly voice said in my ear. "Let me get you out of the middle. If you're not going to dance, you'll get trampled." The creature set me down against the wall of my living room, then charged into the gyrating mass of bodies small and large, his huge feet careful not to step on anything or anyone. "Bigfoot," I whispered.

The music was unearthly, more discordant than tuneful, with lots of whistling and wailing. I suppose you had to have fairy ears to truly appreciate it.

"Yes, it's not being played for you, human," a husky voice said from just over my left shoulder. "Otherwise, you would be entranced and unable to stop dancing." I turned my head and saw a diminutive woman, clad in what looked like spider webs, held aloft by tiny wings churning the air like those of a hummingbird.

The unexpectedly deep voice continued, "Your roommate said we had to be polite to you." She smirked. "Of course, if you'd like us to play for you…."

"Oh, no, that's all right. Thank you. I'm not much of a dancer." Which was true, though the Incomparable Sandy has decreed that I will learn.

"Then I'll leave you, though you don't know what you're missing." With that, the fairy, for such I supposed her to be, flew off into the middle of the rave.

I don't know how long the music and dancing continued. I dared not budge from where the Sasquatch had placed me for fear of inadvertently making a misstep and hurting, or worse, angering one of these strange beings. Or maybe all of them.

I wished I had my house back.

Eventually, sometime in the early afternoon, they began to disappear. I suppose even fairies get tired. First in ones and twos, and then in larger and larger groups, they vanished, and the music faded away. Seeing a clear path, I staggered forward and collapsed onto the sofa. A minute later, the Green Man sat down next to me, his eyes glowing with pleasure. (Again, no metaphor. They were actually glowing.) "That was fun, roomie. Did you enjoy yourself?"

"Uh, well…" I looked about, but amazingly, everything was the same as before. Nothing had been damaged or moved.

He laughed. "Magic, roomie! And the fairies absolutely loved my tree!" He leaned over and whispered in my ear as he had done before. "Personally, I think they were jealous. One even said she didn't think I had it in me! Ha!" He leaned back. "Fun times. Better than the forest, that's for sure." He slapped my leg. "Thanks for cutting me down and bringing me here. I didn't know how much fun this Christmas thing could be!"

I couldn't think of a remark. Frankly, I was exhausted and overwhelmed. Had it only been this morning that the Green Man had shown up?

"The nice thing is, everyone said they could come back tomorrow! Isn't that great?"

I sat up and stared at him in horror. "No. No, no, no, no, no! Once was enough. No tomorrow. No day after tomorrow. I have a life to lead, things to do, and fairy raves aren't part of it."

"Oh, don't worry, roomie. You get on about your life, and we'll just do our thing. You're welcome to join in, of course, but if you're feeling this way, it might be better for you to stay elsewhere."

"What? You're throwing me out of my home?"

"Not if you don't want to go. Certainly not the way you threw me out of mine. Besides, it's only until after Christmas and you get rid of my tree."

"You mean, you and your…friends…are planning to party every day between now and Christmas?"

"Of course. What's a holiday without parties?"

I jumped up and faced him. "No! I won't allow it. It's my house. You're just a visitor, and an ill-behaved one, at that."

"Let me remind you, I didn't choose to come here."

"I know. I know. You've made your point about that. And I'm sorry. If I'd known, I'd have picked another tree…"

"And dispossessed another tree spirit, one of my brothers or sisters? Really? I've been very understanding and accommodating compared to some of them. If you think you've had problems with me, well, let me warn you…." He shook his head, a look of horror passing over his features. "You really have no idea."

"Like I said, I'm sorry. I didn't know. But here we are. If we're going to be together, then we must reach some accommodation. We have to respect each other's needs."

He reached up and took my hand, shaking it. "I totally agree, roomie. Have I asked for anything else? I'm open to negotiating." He took his hand back and put it under his chin, looking as if he were deep in thought. Frankly, I was deep in panic. "I know," he said. "We'll do a rave a day, but I'll limit the number of fairies who can come. No big open house like today."

"No. No more raves. No more fairies."

He frowned. "Come on. Be reasonable. You're not negotiating. Have I told you that you can't have *your* friends in for a party?"

"My friends don't have wings, horns, and blue or green skin."

"Humpff. There you go with the color thing again. Are you sure you're not racist? I tell you what. I'm sorry I had a party with my friends and you felt left out. Let's invite Sandy over and have another party."

"What? No! I...." I was interrupted by my phone ringing in my pocket. I pulled it out and saw that it was the Incomparable Sandy on the other end. I hit the answer button and said, "Hello?"

"Oh, Jack. Thank you for the invitation to come over for dinner tonight and to see your tree. I've been wanting to see what you've done with it."

"Wait. What?"

"Oh, silly. You just texted me an invitation. I can hardly wait. See you in an hour!"

"No, Sandy, wait..." but it was too late. She had hung up. I turned to see a smug smile on my "roommate's" face. "Did you do that?"

"You need to loosen up, Jack, or you'll end up a dull boy. I'm not selfish. I'll even cook dinner. I'm sure the fairies have some terrific recipes."

I stomped about, waving my hands in the air. I was upset, and my hands didn't know what else to do. Well, actually, they did, but I didn't think throttling a tree spirit was the wisest course of action. "I don't want a fairy dinner! I don't want Sandy coming over while you're here."

"Then we need to negotiate, don't we? A rave a day, every day? It's not asking too much."

"Absolutely not! You will not rule this house!" I turned away from him. I couldn't stand to see his incomparably handsome face, not without wanting to smash it in.

"Well, then I guess I'll have to let Sandy see me." It was a wholly new voice that came from behind me, smokey and sexy. I whirled around. There, seated on the sofa, was a woman. A beautiful woman. A woman without horns or green skin, with lush, flowing hair, with abundant curves. An incomparable woman. All I could think of was Jessica Rabbit in the movie saying, "I'm not bad. I'm just drawn this way!" If I had been a cartoon character, I think my eyes would have bugged out of my head.

"Who…who are you?"

"Why, I'm your roomie, of course. Didn't I tell you I can shapeshift? All spirits can, you know." She provocatively uncrossed and then recrossed her impossibly gorgeous legs. "It's a trip, isn't it?"

I knew I couldn't let my Sandy see this…this woman here, especially claiming to be my roommate. I could kiss my proposal goodbye. Then, I remembered, and I laughed. "It's a good trick, but I'm the only one that can see you. Right? It doesn't matter what you look like. Sandy can't see you."

She smiled and slowly winked an eye at me while brushing back a lock of hair from her face. "Are you sure, roomie? I can do lots of things with magic. Do you want to bet your love life on it?"

I was stymied, and she knew it. How could I compete with magic?

"Best make up your mind quickly, bro, while there's still time for me to make dinner. A rave a day, with all my friends?"

It broke my heart, but I knew what I had to do. I walked across the room to where the beautiful tree stood. Reaching down, I hoisted it out of its stand so that it fell over onto the floor. As it did so, somehow the magic was disrupted and suddenly, it was just an ordinary tree again.

"What are you doing, bro?" The sexy voice had changed, and I could see from the corner of my eye that the tree spirit was back, looking his usual green self.

"What I should have done when you first showed up. I'm getting rid of this tree."

He laughed. "It won't work, you know. You can't just toss the tree out into some dump. You can't even take it out and burn it. I'll still be here as your house spirit. The only way to be free of me is to take me back to my forest."

"Then that's what I'll do." It had been a long and tiring trip getting the tree here, but by God, I wasn't going to have my life tyrannized by a tree. I went out to my garage and got some new netting. Carefully, I rolled the tree onto it and tied it up in a bundle. "You could help me, you know," I said to the Green Man, who was still sitting on the couch watching all my efforts.

"No. You got me here, you have to get me back. Like I said, karma, man."

"Karma, sharma," I muttered as I dragged the tree out to my truck. "Anything to get rid of you, man!" It took a bit of doing, especially with the Green Man, who followed me outside, leaning against the house and watching my efforts. Finally, I had it in the truck, tucked in next to my snowmobile. There was one more thing I had to do.

I tapped Sandy's picture on my cell phone. I could hear her phone ringing, then she answered. "Sandy," I said, "I apologize, but something has come up. I can't do dinner tonight. Can we do it tomorrow night?" I held my breath, turning my head to look at the tree spirit. He grinned and nodded at me. Magic.

"Of course, Jack. Tomorrow it is. I'll look forward to it."

"Thank you. You're incomparable!"

As she hung up, the Green Man disappeared.

It took me the rest of the day and into the night, but I got that damn tree back to where I'd cut it down. That's where I left it. I never wanted to see it, or its spirit, again. Heck, I didn't want to see any spirit again.

Driving home, I called my friend, Tom, and asked him where he'd gotten his artificial tree. "Amazon," he said.

Of course.

****

The Green Man looked at his tree lying in the snow. "You did it," came a deep voice from the forest around him. Out from amongst the trees strode another Green Man, this one four times the size of the tree spirit.

"Yes, Chief. Plan 'Insufferable Obnoxious Roommate' worked. The human couldn't take it, just as we expected." The spirit chuckled. "I imagine he's learned a lesson, too."

"Then let's get this home planted again." There was a burst of green light, and suddenly, the tree was no longer horizontal in the snow but standing upright, just as it had always been.

The smaller Green Man sighed. "Tarendel will be happy to have his home back again. But no rest for me until after the human Christmas. Who's next on the list? Who else blundered into a fairy forest to find a tree?"

A name and address appeared in his mind, along with an image of a female tree spirit. "Oh, it's Falial's tree, isn't it? I'm sorry. Tell her I should have her home back soon."

And with that, the Green Man, who was not really a tree spirit at all but a fairy field agent of the GIA, the Gaian Intelligence Service, vanished, en route to another human household and another human roommate.

THE DARKEATER

by
David Spangler

THE DARKEATER

The man sat on the park bench, his legs stretched out before him. Nearby, the happy sound of children playing at a playground filled the air, but he seemed oblivious to this. His eyes closed, his face was tilted up to the afternoon sun, looking for all the world like a man relaxedly soaking up warmth and light before the winter night descended.

The truth was otherwise.

While his body was calm—it needed to be, to do what he was doing—his attention was intensely focused. All around him, he could sense invisible currents of energy. Some of these emanated from the land beneath him, some from the trees and plants in the surrounding park, some from the mountains on the horizon. He drew on all of them to fill his inner reservoir of vitality. But what he really sought for the task ahead of him were energies found not in the physical world around him but in the higher spiritual domains of life. There, in realms home to angels, Devas, and Beings even greater than they, were those currents of Light from which he had to draw what he needed to ensure success in his endeavor.

However, today, they were difficult to reach and even harder to hold within his incarnate form. It called on every aspect of his being to open out to touch such lofty frequencies of life and gather into himself what he required.

Not that he lacked practice. From one life to another, he had done this many, many times before. And here in this part of the world at this time of year, with the Solstice and the many human celebrations of Light and rebirth, the expectations and invocations of people drew the higher frequencies of Spirit closer to the human realm.

But this year, it was as if humanity was shrinking into itself in anxiety and despair, pulling away from the very sources of hope and Light that could help. It was as if he had to cast a net into the deepest parts of the ocean to find what he needed, yet the platform on which he stood was drifting into shallower and shallower waters. It forced him to throw that net further and further out to reach his objective.

Still, he felt as if he had succeeded, though the night would prove whether he was correct. There had been times in the past when he had failed. There had been consequences. This year, it seemed to him that those consequences would be greater than ever before. Yet knowing this, he still felt the Light he had been able to gather into himself and now held in readiness would prove to be sufficient.

"Mommy! Mommy, look! That man's all lit up like our Christmas tree!"

The excited tone of a child's voice brought him back to his surroundings. He opened his eyes to see a frazzled-looking young African-American mother carrying a full shopping bag in one hand, a large purse on a strap over her shoulder, and holding with her free hand onto a dark-haired girl with skin the color of the finest milk chocolate, who looked to be about six years old. The girl was pointing at him, and the mother was obviously trying to shush her up and hurry her away to the nearby playground where other children were laughing and climbing around on various slides, swings, and jungle gyms.

She can see my aura, he thought, and just as quickly, he shielded himself so that his energy field would not be visible to simple clairvoyance. As he did so, the child looked surprised, then switched her attention to the sounds of other children playing. Her mother cast him a quick, apologetic look as she followed her daughter to her new object of interest.

Now, that was interesting, he thought. *And not necessarily unusual*. There were many people, he knew, who were clairvoyant and could see subtle phenomena like auras. In the modern world, however, he also knew that many of them kept quiet about their ability, not wanting to be thought crazy or subjected to ridicule. People now were so sure that the only reality was the one they could perceive through their five senses. *If only they knew how vast and alive and wondrous the world really was.*

Looking at his watch, he realized that it was getting late. He needed to get back to his apartment and prepare. His time in the park, which offered at least some connection to the natural world, had been helpful. He just had to hope it had been sufficient to meet what he knew was coming.

As he started to walk home, he glanced over at the playground. He caught a glimpse of the little dark-haired girl clambering up to the top of a jungle gym. He would have liked to have met her and gotten a sense of her abilities. Were her parents supportive or were they trying to convince her that what she saw was only her imagination? So many people lost or suppressed their native clairvoyance in the face of family disbelief and scorn. Could he have helped her and her parents in some way to recognize and develop her inner Sight? He would never know.

Suddenly, there was a cry and a blur of motion. Stunned, he realized the child had fallen. Almost immediately, the child's mother was plunging into the yelling, scattering crowd of children, her scream rising above all the others. Before he even thought about it consciously, his body was in motion, running towards the playground. *What am I doing?* he thought, but he was there, pushing his way through the converging parents, vaguely aware of people yelling to call 911. Then, he burst up to where the child lay on the ground, her screaming mother bending over her but afraid to touch her for fear of doing more damage. From where he stood, he could see two things clearly. One was that the girl's head was at an unnatural angle on her neck, and the second was that the girl's soul was standing over the body, looking directly at him, compelling him forward.

He caught his breath. This was a rare soul, indeed, its energy field a coruscating wonder of Light and color. An advanced soul, one whose destiny most surely did not include dying on a playground at the age of six.

As if to confirm this, the soul pointed at him, her presence resonating in his mind with a message voiced less in words than in meaning and imagery. "I need your help. My incarnate self feels our power and deems herself more capable than she yet is. She takes risks, and this is the result. But it is not my wish to leave this world with my work undone. You can help me heal my body. But we must act quickly. The Cord of Life is intact but rapidly disintegrating."

In response, he thought, *I must conserve my energy for my own task. I cannot risk failure tonight.* Yet, in that moment, he knew he could not deny this soul its request.

Stepping forward, he leant over the girl. "I'm a doctor," he said to her mother and to any others who might be listening. "Let me examine her."

"She's dead, isn't she! My little Holly is dead!" the woman sobbed, reaching for the body.

"No," he said, gently taking her hands. "Not yet. Let me examine her first." He laid his hands on her neck as if feeling the wound. The bone was indeed broken. Reaching into his own reservoir of Light, he reached out to link with the girl's soul, whose own Light still bathed the body, keeping the Cord of Life from fully disintegrating and disconnecting the soul from the body. His eyes closed, he drew to himself the etheric pattern of the child's healthy body, impressing its structure onto the broken neck. As he and the girl's soul jointly poured the healing energy of Light into her neck, bone and muscle dissolved for a moment then resolidified in their rightful, healed state.

He sighed. His part was done. The soul and the body elemental could now enable the damaged cells to repair. With rest, all would be well, but the soul would have learned not to impress its power so fully or so quickly into its incarnation while its body was still young and forming.

He sat back on his heels and looked at the mother. "Your daughter's fine. She twisted her neck, and the muscles are bruised, but no bones are broken. She's young and should heal and be fine in no time."

"Oh God, thank you! Thank you!" The mother's face was a combination of relief and disbelief. Then, in wonderment, she said, "You healed her. You brought her back." It was not a question. "I saw it."

"No," he replied. He knew he should not attract attention to himself. "There was no need. She never left. Now, she'll heal herself. Just be gentle with her. Her neck will be painful for awhile." He saw that she wanted to say more, to question him more, and he wondered if clairvoyance ran in this woman's family. But then, he heard a commotion behind him as a team of paramedics arrived. Gratefully, he stood up and backed into the crowd as the professionals took over. While no one was watching, he blended into the growing shadows and made his way out of the park.

As he walked home to his apartment building, he felt exhilarated and filled with gratitude at being at the right place at the right time to be of service. He felt that he had lost nothing but had gained energy instead. Contrasted with his misgivings earlier in the day, he now felt hopeful about the night's proceedings. A rising confidence buoyed his step.

That confidence remained throughout the evening. He had a light supper, then rested in his study, reading a favorite book of poems. Off in a corner, a Christmas tree, sparkling with lights and ornaments, reminded him of the little girl and her clairvoyant vision of him. He wondered how she was doing.

As midnight approached, he could feel the Darkness massing. Like seeing black thunderclouds massing on a horizon, he knew that what was coming would be powerful, perhaps more so than ever before. Even though he had faced this before in many lives, sometimes as a man, sometimes as a woman, it still made him nervous and, he had to admit, a little afraid. A person would be a fool to feel otherwise.

In medieval Wales, there had been sin-eaters, men and women who thought they could take into themselves the sins of a person newly dead by eating a ritual meal over their corpse. This, they believed, would cleanse the soul and ease its passage into heaven. He was no sin-eater and had never been in any of his lives, but what he, and others like him around the world, did was similar. *We eat the collective Darkness that humanity has accumulated throughout the preceding year,* he thought. Not all the Darkness, or even most of it! No, that would be beyond any mortal. *But enough of it that humanity might enter the new year less burdened and with more hope than otherwise.*

He remembered how it had started for him. It had been in the Fifteenth Century in Moorish North Africa. There, deep in the Atlas mountains of Morocco, in a small cave whose walls were embedded with amethyst crystals that reflected torchlight like a thousand jeweled stars, he had been initiated into a spiritual Order whose calling was to shepherd and protect humanity along its evolutionary path. Throughout his various lifetimes, he had sought to fulfill this calling as best he could, eventually becoming, as had some others in the Order, a Darkeater. He then was one who drew the negative and hurtful energies generated by human thought and behavior into himself, consuming and transmuting them through the Light that he could hold within his spirit.

This was something he did on a small scale all the time, whenever and wherever the need presented itself. But once a year, during the longest night, humanity's collective Darkness rose like a tide seeking redemption. That was when he and the Darkeaters like him would step into that tide, seeking to transmute as much as they could.

The clock on the mantle of his fireplace chimed. Midnight had come. The time for remembering was over. The Darkness was waiting.

Using a mantra he had been given over five hundred years earlier in his initiation, remembered in life after life, he shifted into an altered state, opening a well of Light within himself. With that Light, he reached out to the subtle life in the room around him, the spirit within the matter of which all things are composed. He wove webs of connection and love with the things around him, creating a grail of energy. He then expanded his inner well of Light into that larger grail space, making his entire room a chalice to hold the Light he would invoke.

With this done, he reached outward to the Presences of Light attuned to his Order, drawing their Light into the room and into himself. When this was done, he opened this grail to the collective pain of humanity.

And the Darkness flowed in, filling the room, filling his body, filling his consciousness.

At first, it was waves of surface anxiety. So many things were causing uncertainty and fear. The ongoing pandemic. The climate crisis. Political upheavals. Wars. Economic dislocation and loss. Racial divisions. Oppression. Injustice. Hatred.

The hurtful energies arising from these causes were challenging but he knew how to deal with them. In one way or another, he faced many of them every day in the impoverished neighborhoods where he lived and worked, though at a much lesser scale. He knew how to draw them into the Light, remaining neutral, not taking sides, not giving the negativity any opportunity to hook into him. He knew how to stand in love, funneling the hurtful and hurting energies into the deeper places of Spirit where healing and reformation would take place.

The challenge was that there was so much of it, and it kept coming. People were feeling lost, alone, vulnerable, and there were predators, both human and metaphysical, that could and did take advantage of this, stoking and feeding on the fears that divisions created. As the hours wore on, he could feel his endurance being tested. With a flash of dismay, he realized that the healing he had done earlier in the day for the little girl had in fact drained his reserves. His energy was not as full and strong as he had thought.

I should have let the matter alone, he thought. But he realized that he could not have done differently. A soul in need had summoned him. He had had no choice but to respond. To have done otherwise would have violated the oath of his initiation to serve, to protect, and to shepherd.

As the night deepened, however, he sensed a shift taking place. The nature of the Darkness, of the pain, was changing, the suffering becoming more complex, less easy to parse and transmute. He had expected this. It was often this way. Humanity held profound levels of trauma unresolved from its ancient past. It didn't always surface, and when it did, it was always more intractable to deal with. It was stubborn in its resistance to letting go and being healed.

This night, though, the depth and extent of the trauma-shaped energies was more than he had faced before. Why this was so, he didn't know for sure, though he had suspicions. Certainly, there were more people in the world than in the past, more places for suffering to take place and trauma to be experienced. The challenges humanity was facing were global and systemic in nature. Human beings had a greater sense of themselves as a planetary species than ever before. The awareness of suffering overlapped boundaries of place and time that had once kept it broken up into regions and localities as in earlier times. Humanity groaned in unison.

But this also meant it could hope in unison, aspire in unison, perhaps in time even love in unison. Awakening to its planethood was a necessary step for humanity, but in the process, trauma was more deeply and universally experienced, and its ancient roots more exposed.

Whatever the reason, he now found himself facing deep trauma that gnawed away at identity and spirit, a black hole of spirit sucking everything into itself, into its pain and incomprehension. It might be collective in nature, but he experienced it as millions of voices crying out, men, women, and worst of all, children.

Through sheer force of intention and love, he sought to hold the integrity of the grail space around him, the energetic weave that held a sacred force of healing and redemption. But he could feel the weave unraveling. He could feel the space shrinking, connections dissolving. The boundaries were failing.

I am Love, he thought. *I am Light. I can eat the Dark and turn it into Light. I am Love. I am Light.*

Over and over, he kept repeating this to himself, holding his mind and heart open to the pain. He knew if he could just hold on, the night would end, the dawn would come, and with it, the Angel of the Dawn who always came then to hold and restore him.

But pain had long since turned into horror and anguish into depravity. Deep in the trauma was the lust for power, the power to inflict pain, to divide, to dominate, and thus to be safe. Safe from the challenges of incarnation. Safe from the challenges of this world. Safe from the demands of evolution. It was no longer a collective energy he dealt with but a presence, the Darkness taking on will and purpose to defend itself, to extend itself, to be all that is.

Never before had this presence made itself so known to him. It was a parasite in the body of humanity, one that had fed and grown fat on the suffering it induced. It was a parasite of fear, its tendrils everywhere. He had no doubt it must be exposed to the Light, for the protection of humankind if not also for its own healing. But this exposure was more than he had bargained for, more than he had energy for.

He could feel the grail of power and support around him shatter. He could feel his connection to the angels of his Order obscured. He was driven into himself, into his own Self-Light, and it was not enough. He was not enough. He had never been enough.

NO! He thought. This is the voice of the Darkness itself, attacking his resolve, his confidence, his very sense of self. He *could* hold. He *would* hold. He would hold this dark presence to the Light.

But he could feel his body weakening. He had failed before, trying to eat the Dark. When he had, it took him days, weeks, sometimes months to recover. In one life, he had even died. *That is what is happening now*, he thought. *I will hold to the end, but I will not survive. It is too much.*

He felt lost in the midst of Darkness. *I cannot eat this Dark. It has eaten me*, he thought in despair. *I am alone.*

Suddenly, he heard a presence in his mind. "You are NOT alone," it said. It sounded familiar. Was it another one of his Order, come to help? But it did not feel that way. It didn't carry the energy signature that one of his fellow initiates would have had. *But who...?*

Then, he recognized it. It was the presence of the soul of the little girl whose body he had helped heal the day before. And with that recognition, he felt hands on his body. "You...you should not be here," he said out loud. "Danger." For he knew above all else that abusing and damaging children was close to the heart of the traumatized Darkness. He had seen too many visions of this during the night.

"No, I am not in danger," came the reply, and with it came the feeling of many hands touching him, infusing him with energy. "We are many, but we act as one. We have come to live on earth at this time to help Humanity step forward out of Darkness, into Light, into wholeness."

Another voice said, "We are all Lightbearers. We are all your children."

A third voice added its note. "We felt your need. We came to help, as you helped one of us."

"Now," said a fourth, "you have done enough for this night. The Darkness has not triumphed. Sleep now. The Angel of the Dawn is coming to be with you."

And with that, consciousness fled him, and he slept.

He came to feeling his body stretched out on his sofa and his head cradled in a soft lap. *It's the Angel,* he thought. *The dawn has come. The longest night is over. I survived.*

Then he felt something different. It was soft, like down, but tickling his neck. *What is that? A beard?*

He opened his eyes and discovered that he was lying with his head in the lap of Santa Claus. He didn't have the energy, or, for that matter, the desire, to move, but he said, "You look different. You've never been Santa before."

The angel smiled, its eyes twinkling behind rimless spectacles. "It seemed appropriate. What is Santa but the Hope in the hearts of children, the very hope the Darkness seeks to extinguish."

"The hope the world needs." He remembered his ordeal in the night. "It seems it was children who saved me."

"Indeed," said the Santa angel. "Children always save us, if we let them." The angel glanced over towards the Christmas tree in the corner of the room and smiled. "There are no presents under your tree. What would you like Santa to bring you?"

The Darkeater smiled back. "An hour's nap here on Santa's lap would be nice." He closed his eyes.

"Then so let it be done."

And it was.

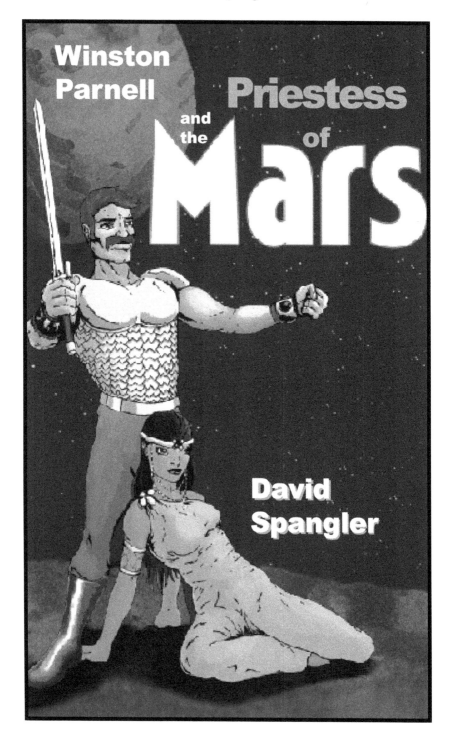

WINSTON PARNELL
&
THE PRIESTESS OF MARS

It was a dark and foggy night in old London town. It was a week before Christmas. Winston Parnell and I were snug like bugs in our flat in the mews off Crystalberry Lane. It was so foggy you couldn't even step outside because you couldn't find the outside to step into! But Winston and I were all cozied up. There was a fire in the hearth casting a cheery glow over the room. In one corner, the play of light from the flames made the faces carved on the old Haida totem pole seem to smile and wink. It was a memento from one of our adventures in the British Northwest where Winston had solved the puzzling case of the raven-headed man. Hanging next to it was one of the grinning masks from New Guinea that Winston insisted on having on display but which I found hideous, partly because it reminded me of the spear wound I'd taken on *that* adventure. Other smaller artifacts were scattered about the room, from fossils from the Atlas Mountains which millions of years ago had been on the bottom of the sea to bits of statuary from long-lost cities buried in Saharan sands or the jungles of Central America, all testifying to the life of danger and travel that a man would lead associating with Winston Parnell.

And yes, of course, there was a Christmas tree in one corner, opposite the totem. Christmas was, after all, very near, and while frankly for Winston one day was much like another, I had always kept the Yule faithfully and with much merriment. Indeed, I had on more than one occasion seen the Mystery—the one we all know as Santa Claus—making his annual appearance.

Winston himself was reading some new scientific paper, puffing on his big pipe, and humming to himself, which he sometimes did when he was deep in thought. I had been reading a letter from one of my sonswho was serving in one of the colonial regiments stationed near Mount Olympus on Mars. He had written to describe a Martian legend that was their version of Christmas. In his letter, he had made a sketch of a Martian goddess who, he said, was a kind of Mother Christmas, except that she took things, rather than giving them. "Not my idea of Christmas," I thought, as I folded the letter and put it in my pocket. I picked up the *Gazette*. There was more unrest in the Martian colonies. A vote in Parliament over the fate of the colonies had nearly brought down the present government. And as I recall, on top of all that, some scandal had erupted in the Foreign Office, but then scandals were always erupting there. How Her Majesty ever expected to run an empire with the men she had.... Well, never mind about that.

An article in the middle of the paper caught my eye. "I say, Winston," I said, looking it over. "There's a professor from Harvard who claims Martians invaded earth thousands of years ago."

The humming stopped. "How does he know this?" my friend asked.

"He claims recent findings on Mars suggest an expedition was led against this planet ten thousand or so years ago, about the time Plato suggests Atlantis fell. He claims the fall of Atlantis was due to alien invasion. What poppycock! Even if Atlantis ever existed, which I doubt, the Martians are savages. They could hardly have crossed interstellar space and invaded us."

"Ah, but my dear fellow, they were not always as they seem now. There are many ruins on that world that suggest a great civilization once flourished there. And as for Atlantis, remember that adventure we had in the Bahamas? There were strange things indeed upon that uncharted island in the Atlantic."

"Even so...."

But at that moment, what promised to be an interesting conversation, at least for me, was interrupted by a knock at the front door downstairs.

"Good God!" I exclaimed, "Who could be out on a night like this?"

"Someone with urgent business, I expect," Winston replied,

his deep voice quickening with interest, undoubtedly relieved not to be debating the merits of Atlantis or ancient Martian invasions with me. He hated speculations. "Someone from the Palace, no doubt."

"The Palace? But really, Winston, how could even you know that?"

"Elementary, my dear Arthur. No ordinary person would seek us out on a night like this, just as you say. If someone has made the trouble, it will be over a matter of extreme importance, and that means either the Ministry or the Palace. But the Ministry's all stirred up over the latest infidelities, and I doubt they need my services for that. Simple elimination, my good man. But hark!" We heard the squeaking of the front door being opened and soft voices coming up the stairs. "We'll know in a minute. Our good Mrs. Baker has let him in." Winston put down his pipe and magazine and leapt to his feet to be ready to greet the unknown visitor.

Indeed, no more than a minute passed before we heard footsteps mounting the stairs and our housekeeper, Mrs. Baker, poked her head in the door to the study. "Sorry to bother, gen'lemen, but 'ere's a visitor for you."

"By all means, show the gentleman in, Mrs. Baker," Winston said. Our housekeeper stood to one side and a distinguished-looking man dressed in top hat and a black cloak with dark trousers and shoes showing underneath stepped into the room. He looked to be middle aged, perhaps in his late forties. He removed his cloak and his hat and gave them to Mrs. Baker, giving her a smile and making a slight bow as he did so. He wore a dark jacket over a light vest and shirt, the collar of which had a small, unfamiliar pin stuck into it. His hair was darkish brown with flecks of grey above the temples. His face was not unhandsome by any means, but he would not necessarily have stood out in a crowd.

He stepped forward and offered Winston his hand. "My name is Roger Colliston," he said, his voice rich and cultured. "I am delighted you would see me on such a beastly night, Mr. Parnell.

I assure you it will not be a waste of your time."

My friend shook the other's hand and nodded his head slightly in agreement. "I'm sure it won't be, Mr. Colliston. And this is my colleague, Arthur Matthews."

He turned and took my hand as well. His grip was sure and firm and bespoke a man with a military background. "A privilege," he said. Then he turned back to Winston. "My mission is important and delicate in the extreme," he said.

"I quite understand. What you would say to me, you may say to Arthur. He is discretion's obedient servant."

"Then I am in good hands," Colliston said.

"Here," I said, indicating the easy chair in which I had but lately been happily seated. "Please sit down."

"Thank you." He sat down, and I could not help but notice a fluidity and grace to his movements. I also remarked that for a man apparently on a mission of some importance and urgency, he seemed preternaturally calm and composed. I pulled up another chair and sat as well. Winston reclaimed his seat and his pipe, stuffing shag in the latter and tamping it down as he fixed our visitor with piercing grey eyes that I knew were missing nothing.

"Before you begin," he said, applying match to pipe and puffing until the tobacco was satisfactorily lit, "let me tell you what I already know. You come to me from the Palace, but you are not part of the household staff. You are instead a friend of His Royal Highness, the Prince of Wales. You are also a Lodge Adept, undoubtedly one of high degree in the ranks of the Holy Fraternity of Albion, and you have been in ritual work tonight. Indeed, I would venture to say that the matter at hand has some occult origin to it, something revealed to you only within the hour, the significance and urgency of which brought you to my chambers. Further, it is not a governmental or political matter but a problem of the Throne."

While Winston delivered his observations, I watched the

face of our visitor. Many had ascribed magical powers to my friend, so astonished were they at what he revealed about them. But I knew it was merely—dare I say *merely?*—the results of his keen observation and brilliant intellect, a formidable combination that must in truth seem miraculous to the ordinary mortal. I was impressed, though, that rather than the usual expressions of incredulity and then wonder and surprise that played upon the faces of most of our visitors at such moments, Colliston's face remained imperturbable with only a slight widening of his eyes to indicate any reaction at all.

"Your reputation is more than well deserved, Mr. Parnell," our visitor said, leaning forward in his chair. "You are correct in every particular. I had not realized that in addition to your many gifts you were psychically endowed as well."

Winston smiled. "I'm afraid I am not so blessed...or cursed as the case might be. I have no unusual powers, Mr. Colliston, only a keen eye, an attentive mind, and a modest capacity for deduction."

"Ah, then I *am* impressed. Would that many of my colleagues could say the same thing, for then we would be a more powerful Lodge than we are. Attention and careful reasoning are the hallmark of a successful adept as well."

"Indeed." Winston puffed on his pipe.

"But as you deny any of the fey arts, before I tell you what the issue is, I must ask how you came to know the things you just said. I thought you were using inner sight."

"No, ordinary vision suffices. As I told Arthur when we heard you knock, I was sure you were from the Palace as I could conceive no other agency that would send someone abroad to meet with me so late on such a night as this, or no other representative so dedicated and loyal as to venture forth in such a fog except on behalf of the Throne. When you shook my hand, this was confirmed for me, for I noticed your cufflinks were those made especially by the Prince of Wales as gifts for his closest friends. Yet, you are not part of the Palace household. For one thing the cut of your clothes is individual and unique, obviously expressing a degree of personal style I would not expect to find in a staff person, not to mention the obvious quality and expense of the material."

"And the Lodge connection? Or that I have lately come from a ritual working of some importance?"

"Elementary." Winston pointed to the pin in our visitor's collar. "This little object tells me much." As he spoke, Colliston's hand went up and touched, then removed the object. A wry smile passed over his face. "This is a device worn by Lodge members of a certain degree and then only during rituals. It is, I believe, a marker that allows you to pass the Perilous Threshold into the space of the working itself."

"How do you know that? Such knowledge is reserved as secret within the highest reaches of the Lodge. You must be a Lodgeman yourself."

"No, I am not, but I am interested in all things and my eyes and ears are always open. There is no end to the knowledge you can gain in life with these as allies."

"Incredible!"

"But be at ease, Colliston. Your Lodge secrets are safe with Arthur and me. As I have said, we worship at discretion's altar. At any rate, seeing this pin told me two things, first that you belonged to a Lodge and had been working a ritual, otherwise you would not have been wearing this device upon your person, and second, that whatever you discovered had borne itself upon you with such urgency and terribleness that it preoccupied your mind, causing you to forget to remove this pin before you rushed from the temple to come here."

"Astounding!"

"Further, in spite of the urgency and importance of the matter, enough to cause such a lapse of concentration as to forget to remove all your ritual regalia and to bring you here at late hours in the worst fog in decades, you present a calm and composed demeanor. I have seen such before with the monks of Gautama the Buddha in the Far East, men who have achieved such inner peace and knowledge as to render them invulnerable to the shocks of life. But I rarely see this in the West where many of the disciplines of the Eastern adepts are as yet unknown or at least not widely practiced. Except," and he held up a finger to make his point, "except with Lodge adepts of a high degree. A very high degree, I should add."

"I can see as you explain it, there is no need for psychic abilities to grasp these things, only a remarkable mind. And I can see that once you knew of my connection with His Royal Highness, you could safely assume we were fraternal brothers and part of the royal Lodge together."

"That was my assumption. And it is correct as far as it goes, I'm sure. But that is not your home Lodge, is it?"

Colliston went still and quiet. "I don't understand. A man usually only belongs to one Lodge if he belongs to any."

"I agree, if he is a man."

"Good God, Winston, are you saying Colliston here is not a man? Not human?"

Winston smiled. "Oh, I'm sure he is as human as you or I, Arthur, but he is more than a man. He is a Master Adept of the Inner Lodge, the Planetary Lodge."

Colliston smiled, his eyes flashing, and for a brief moment I thought I saw a man carved from living Light sitting in the chair, but I blinked, and he was as he had been before, an ordinary but distinguished man sitting before me.

Winston nodded. "I thought so," he said. "I am honored."

"Oh, the honor is all mine," Colliston said. "Let them who have eyes to see and all that, but it's rare that someone *can* see or does. How did you know?"

"Several things told me. For one thing, how did you come here? I heard no sound of horses' hooves on the cobblestones outside and no sound of any other conveyance. Nor did I hear footsteps. And I have, I assure you, exceptional hearing. And when you arrived at our chambers, your hat and cloak were dry, not moist as they would have been had you spent any time at all out in the foggy air. Further your shoes are dry. I concluded, therefore, that you had apported yourself to our premises, though from where I could not say. With this thought, I asked myself, "Who would have the power to move from one place to another without crossing the intervening space?"

"Angels," I said. "An angel could do it, or someone carried by an angel."

"An angel could indeed do so, Arthur, but there are phenomena that accompany the movement and presence of angels…"

"Yes…" I said, "such as a burst of Light or a feeling of warmth."

"I saw no such light out our window, which overlooks the front door, and while the fire is a cheery and warm companion, it is not an angel's heat. No, this was no angelic phenomenon at work," Winston continued, obviously enjoying himself. "And having ascertained that, I asked myself, who or what manner of person might do what an angel could. And though I'm not a Lodgeman myself nor into magic or the esoteric arts, I am, as I say, an interested and curious fellow, so I have learned that certain persons are able to perform such feats."

"The Masters of the Inner Lodge," I said. "Human beings so evolved in spiritual and moral powers as to become superhuman."

"Even so. Am I not right, Colliston, or whatever your true name is?"

Our visitor nodded his head. "Oh, I am Roger Colliston right enough, and you are correct. Though, Mr. Matthews," he said, turning to me, "I would not say 'superhuman' but merely fulfilling the promise given to all human beings by the Creator."

"I take it you are not the age you look," Winston said.

"I am four hundred years old," he said. "I took my initiation into planetary adeptship in 1632, at the age of fifty. I was living at the time in the Virginia colony in the Americas. That, I believe, is the homeland of your mother, though your father is English."

Winston nodded.

"The one who initiated me was a native medicine man, a most powerful individual who had seen Cortez burn the cities of the Aztecs."

"Good God," I exclaimed, still hardly able to believe it, yet somehow believing it.

Winston gestured with his pipe. "That pin. That was a bit of misdirection intended for me, with just enough truth to it to lead me to an erroneous conclusion that you were a highly placed but distraught Lodgeman. That you would leave such an important bit of ritual regalia forgotten on your collar was too incredible for me to believe, knowing the discipline and presence of mind you must have to work your rituals. Likewise, the cufflinks. You wished me to think that you are part of the Royal Lodge and here with the authority, or at least the tacit knowledge, of the Palace behind you."

"You truly are the Master here, Mr. Parnell, for you have uncovered all my secrets and more than proven to me that you are the one we need."

"Ah, but that is where I am stumped," Winston said. "Given who—and what—you are and the powers you command, why would you require one such as I? Whatever has happened, surely you and your colleagues in the Inner Lodge are more than adequate to handle it?"

Colliston frowned. "As I said to Mr. Matthews, we are not superhumans, able to bend anything to our will. We are evolved beyond the normal cut of humankind, this is true, but we are not all-powerful. Though I could do some of the things you do, I would do so through psychic means rather than through the power of deductive reasoning and logic such as you use. You are without parallel, Mr. Parnell. And that is why I come to you. You see, while you were right about the pin—I did not forget it but put it there deliberately to see what you would deduce—you were also right that I had come here straight from ritual work, in which I did uncover the most serious of circumstances. And I *am* here on behalf of the Throne, and the Prince's Lodge *is* my outer Lodge."

Colliston sighed and for the first time since he had arrived, he looked disturbed. "Again, Mr. Parnell and Mr. Matthews, I must ask for your absolute discretion. What I am about to reveal is of the highest secrecy. Only His Royal Highness and his mother, the Queen, are aware of it in the Palace. Indeed, it was he who contacted me and made me aware of what had happened, though I would have known soon enough. As yet no Lodgeman or Churchman knows. Only my colleagues in the Planetary Lodge."

"Do you wish an oath from us for our silence?"

He paused as if considering. "No. I have no right to bind your souls in that way. I shall trust in the nobility and strength of your characters in this matter." When he said this, I could see Winston straighten up somewhat, and I confess, even I felt somehow ennobled and better for the regard in which he held us. It is said that the high adepts of the Lodges, like the high Ecclesiasts of the Church, can truly read a man's or woman's soul and know its weaknesses and virtues. If this man were the Master Adept Winston said he was, and I saw no reason to doubt it, then he had truly judged us and found us worthy in ways no ordinary man could do. It felt good.

"Then come, man! Tell us what has happened." Winston said impatiently. He was like a hound scenting prey and barely restrained by the leash.

"One of the Hallows has been stolen."

"Good God!" Winston exclaimed.

"The Prince of Wales himself was its Guardian," Colliston continued. "He discovered it missing only this morning. He contacted me immediately, and I performed a ritual to discover what had happened. I sought to engage the Planetary Mind itself."

"And did you succeed?"

"No. I was strangely blocked. I could not determine where the Hallow has gone and who has taken it. That is why I have come to you. Perhaps you can do with your talents what I could not with mine."

"I see. You felt nothing?"

"Only something alien, not like anything I have encountered before."

"And the nature of the Hallow?"

Colliston frowned. "I am sorry. I am not at leave to tell you that. Only the Prince can reveal that information to you as its Guardian."

"Deuce it all!" I exclaimed. "You are both speaking gibberish to me. What *are* these Hallows?"

"The Hallows can be many things, my friend," Winston said, "They can be qualities like Honor or Justice, or Courage."

"And more," said Colliston. "Not only qualities but forces of life itself. They are the hearts of those spiritual beings we call the Mysteries, the spiritual Powers who embody and nurture sacred qualities and forces in the world until they can live in the hearts of humanity. They are the seeds of Humanity's future."

I was bewildered. "How can such a thing be threatened, or stolen? How can Courage be nicked away like a common wallet or the family silver?"

"Because the Hallows all have a physical counterpart. They exist partly in the World of Light and partly in this world."

I sat back, dumbfounded.

"It is not easy to steal one, I can assure you. They are hidden and protected in places all over the world. It is the work of the Inner Lodge…"

Winston raised his hand, forestalling further explanation. "I am sure all was done properly, but if a Hallow was stolen, then there is a scene of the crime. And that scene may yield clues. You must take us there immediately. The sooner I can study it, the more likely there will be clues that have survived." He sprang to his feet.

"Dash it, Winston. Wherever we have to go, we're not going to find a cab in this soup tonight," I said.

"No, Arthur. Our friend here will transport us in the manner he himself came here, or is that beyond your ability?"

Colliston smiled. "I think I can handle two of you. But are you ready to leave now?"

"It will take but a moment for Arthur and me to collect what we need. We can travel light."

"Then, if you would be so kind as to have your housekeeper return my hat and coat…"

"Of course. Arthur, would you do the honors? There are one or two things I need to gather up." Winston launched into a whirlwind of activity, racing about the room, throwing on his great overcoat and stuffing things into its many pockets, while I gathered a few items into a backpack. I noticed he buckled on his revolver, so I stuck my trusty Webley into my pocket as well. In the meantime, Mrs. Baker, responding to my calls, arrived on the scene, carrying Colliston's hat and cloak. In moments we were ready.

"You won't need your armament, my brothers," Colliston said.

Winston smiled, and it was a predator's smile. "I understand you cannot take life, but I am under no such prohibition should the need arise and danger threaten. I shall keep my firearm for now."

"To each man his path, then," Colliston replied with good humor. "Stand close to me and take my hands." We crowded next to him, Winston grabbing his right hand, and I his left. "I suggest you close your eyes," he said. I did as he commanded, but even then, a brightness as of the sun pierced through my closed lids. A warmth flooded through me and a feeling of great contentment. Then it was dark again.

I opened my eyes.

We were standing in a moderate-sized room lit only by the flickering light of torches. The walls and ceiling were all carved of stone, while the floor was earth beaten down by who knew how many feet over how many centuries. Along one side was a row of small, stone chests wrapped and sealed with iron bindings. One stood open, its bindings broken. On another side was a large display case. Whatever was in it sparkled brightly in the dim light.

In the middle of the room was a throne carved from a single large piece of stone.

Winston looked about. "The throne...." he started to say, but was interrupted by a strong, manly voice coming from our rear.

"...is where the true coronation takes place of Britain's Kings and Queens."

We whirled about to see His Royal Highness the Prince of Wales entering through a square portal cut into the stone. We immediately made to kneel before him, but he signaled us to remain standing. "As you were," he said. "I have not come to interrupt your work. Your reputations precede you. It is a privilege to meet the famous Winston Parnell and his colleague, Arthur Matthews."

We each bowed our heads in acknowledgement of the compliment. "It is our privilege, Your Highness," Winston replied. Then he pointed to the display case with the glow within it. "The jewels in the case over there, I take it those are the real Crown Jewels?"

The Prince glanced at Colliston, then back at Winston. "Excellent deduction, good fellow! That's correct. The jewels in the Tower are all real and are used in the public ceremonies and coronations. They have all been properly consecrated. But here," and he swept his hand about the room, "here are the real instruments of Power. Here are the Talismans in which the powers of Sovereignty and the Land are embodied."

"When a Monarch takes office," Colliston added, "he or she is crowned in Westminster Abbey for all the people to see. But before that, he or she is brought down here and the true ceremony of investment and initiation into the Mysteries of Sovereignty and Rulership is conducted by the four Heads of the Inner Lodge, one representing the Church, one representing the Lodge, and two representing humanity and the powers of nature. This is where the Queens and Kings of Britain truly receive their power."

"And their burden," said His Royal Highness.

"Part of which is to protect the Hallows of Britain." Winston said, to which the Prince nodded.

Indicating the open chest, Winston said, "And this is where the theft occurred?"

"That is correct," affirmed the Prince. "Do you wish to inspect it?"

"In a moment, Your Highness. First, I want to just look…."

Winston began a slow turn around, and I could see the hawk-like mien come over him as his keen senses and even keener mind took in everything in his surroundings. I had seen him do this many times. He called it "inhabiting the space," and it was as if he pushed the veil of his senses like a bubble out to fill the room, taking note of everything, using his imagination to reconstruct what must have happened when the crime took place. Although he denied any kind of psychic abilities, it was as if he were compelling the very stones and earth to speak to him. Only when he felt fully attuned to the room, I knew, would he turn his attention to the individual details of the chest itself.

The Prince, Colliston, and I, as if by instinct, stepped back to one side of the room, giving the greatest detective and adventurer of our age, perhaps of any age, time and space to do his work.

Finally, Winston turned his attention to the small chest. He advanced towards it slowly, one step at a time, stopping after each movement to scan the area again. I called it his "stalking mode," and he resembled nothing so much as a graceful feline moving towards its prey.

When he reached the chest, he pulled a magnifying glass from one of the pockets in his greatcoat and knelt down. Everything was subjected to the most careful scrutiny while the three of us waited with increasing suspense for what he would discover. Though I knew that the Prince and the Adept must have questions—I certainly did—I also knew they were loath to break the awesome silence that had descended around my friend.

Eventually, Winston stood up and faced us. There was a strange look upon his face, excitement and bewilderment mixed together. His eyes seemed focused upon some scene not in this room, perhaps not even in this universe. Though my friend adamantly swore he was not psychic, I knew he had perceptions beyond the ordinary.

He blinked his eyes, and looked at us, as if just now becoming aware that we were present. "I now know who stole the Hallow and where it is," he announced simply. Then he seemed to gaze off into that other world again, a frown playing upon his brow.

I couldn't bear it anymore. "Well, come on, man," I blurted out. "If you know, then tell us, for God's sake, and end this suspense." I knew I echoed the feelings of His Highness and the Master Adept.

Once more Winston blinked and with an effort of will brought his attention back to the three of us. He bowed slightly in our direction. "My apologies, Your Highness, and my friends. I have had a most extraordinary experience which I am not sure how to interpret. Indeed, I may require *your* assistance in this matter, Colliston." He shook himself slightly, then seemed once more in full possession of himself. "But first, to the matter at hand." He gestured to the chest. "The Hallow was stolen by a Martian from the Northern Highlands, a drone of the K'thar priestly cast, and, I presume, is currently upon the Red Planet itself. Furthermore, the Hallow that was taken is that of Father Christmas, or as he is known in my mother's homeland, Santa Claus."

Silence once more descended upon us. Then, the Prince exclaimed, "Astonishing!" Even I, who had seen Winston perform amazing feats of deduction before, was dumbstruck. But not only by his intellectual prowess. The implications of what he had said were staggering. How had a Martian gained entry to the most secret, the most holy, the most guarded chamber in all of Britain? They were by all accounts a savage and degenerate race, living in the ruins and dregs of a once-great civilization. Even my son, a most tolerant and kindly soul for a soldier, had little use for the natives he'd met in his current billet on the Red Planet. They had no super science that we knew of that would let them travel millions of miles across interstellar space from their world to ours without detection. And of all the Hallows they might have stolen, why Father Christmas?

Colliston was eyeing Winston speculatively. "In spite of what you say, you did not come to these insights entirely deductively, am I right?"

Winston lowered his eyes for a moment as if in momentary doubt, then looked boldly back at the High Adept. "As you say, and I would appreciate your insights in this matter. I seem to have been...there is no other word for it...inspired with certain knowledge."

Colliston chuckled. "Good God, man, it's not a disease! We call it intuition, and every adept prizes it highly. And you, Sir, *are* an adept, even though you are not a Lodgeman and though you may deny it to yourself."

"I am an adept of reasoning and observation, Sir, not of mystical abilities such as yourself."

"That may be by training and inclination, Parnell, but you are human, and all humans are intuitive to some degree and open to the Mind that embraces us all. You have simply been touched by a Higher Power, that's all."

Winston looked for a moment as if he had bitten into a lemon, but then he smiled graciously. "It seems I have no other course but to accept what you say, for there is no denying that certain knowledge came into my mind but in a way divorced from the usual paths of reason."

Colliston chuckled again. "It could hardly be otherwise." He spread his arms wide to encompass the room around us. "This place, filled with the Hallows and the Sovereignty of Britain, is steeped with the most puissant spiritual power in the land. I would have been surprised had a man of your abilities and awareness not been touched in some way."

The Prince cleared his throat. "Gentlemen, this is all well and good, and I appreciate that you've had some kind of unusual experience, Mr. Parnell, but would you kindly now tell me just what you've deduced or been inspired with or however the deuce you have come to the knowledge we need!"

Winston immediately bowed to the Prince. "A thousand pardons, your Highness. Of course." He turned back to the chest. "Discovering it was a Martian was elementary. The perpetrator of this theft left clues to his origins. Observe." He pointed to a bit of dirt lying beside the chest. He picked up a pinch of it between his thumb and forefinger. "This is a bit of sand or soil left behind, perhaps falling off a garment or left by the foot of the thief. At first, I took it for sand but then realized it had characteristics found in volcanic soil. As I studied it through my magnifier, it resembled the soil found on the slopes of the volcanoes in the Sandwich Islands, or as the natives call it, Hawaii. I had reason to become familiar with this particular kind of soil, called *palagonite*, while escaping from being sacrificed to the native goddess Pele some years ago, as you'll remember, Arthur. But it is not identical. Then I remembered a monograph written by Sir Percival Lovelace, the geologist on the first Imperial Mars Expeditionary Landing stating that much Martian soil bore a close geological and chemical resemblance to *palagonite*. From this I deduced that our culprit had either been on Mars or Hawaii prior to this theft."

He reached into a pocket and produced a clear plastic envelope. Carefully he placed the sample of soil within it. "Of course, only detailed microscopic analysis can confirm this deduction, but I am fairly confident about it."

"I see," said the Prince of Wales. "But as you say, the thief could be someone from the Sandwich Isles. Surely, incredible though that itself seems to me, it makes more sense than that an alien savage from millions of miles away somehow gained access to this chamber. Why are you so sure our culprit is a Martian?"

Winston took out his magnifying glass and handed it to the Prince. "Look, Sire, at the edges of the chest and the lid and around the binding. The lock was forced open and the bindings broken by great force or great strength, but not without cost to the perpetrator. See, there and there…"

The Prince looked and then stepped back, handing the magnifying glass to Colliston who looked as well and then handed it to me. Gazing through the lens, I saw splotches of blue and fragments of what looked like blue leather. At first, I had no idea what I was looking at, but then, it became clear. But His Highness announced his conclusions first.

"Blood and skin."

"Indeed," Winston replied. "Blue blood and blue skin of a Martian native. And note the texture and scale patterns of the leather-like skin. That scale pattern is found in natives from the Northern Highlands. And unless I am mistaken, those faint but darker striations are indicators of the striping common to a member of the priestly caste of the K'Thars of the Northern Highlands."

"Brilliant deduction, Parnell," said the Prince of Wales. "But how do you know it was a drone?"

"Elementary, your Highness. Mars is a planet of lesser gravity than ours, so a Martian would be weaker on our planet while one of us, raised in a more powerful gravity field, would be exceptionally strong on theirs. It is an advantage our military has taken full use of, I believe, in quelling native uprisings there and gaining an upper hand. Yet, great strength was used to force open the bindings on this chest. The thief used his bare hands to do so, losing skin and blood in the process. Only a drone would have the strength to perform this feat even when weakened by our gravity."

I realized Winston was right. The Martian natives came in two forms, both blue-skinned. Both were humanoid, but the drones, brutes eight and nine feet in height and bulging with muscles, had four arms and were possessed of superhuman strength. Were it not for the advantages our superior weaponry and technology and the lighter gravity of Mars gave to our soldiers, we would be hard pressed to defeat them in battle, so powerful and savage were they with their great claymore-like swords and battle axes.

"This makes excellent sense, my dear fellow," said Colliston, "but there is still one thing that puzzles me. How did you identify the nature of the Hallows itself? What clue revealed that to you?"

A troubled look passed over Winston's face. "That, Sir, is the knowledge that came to me with no rationale behind it. It sprang full blown into my mind and in a manner that I could not doubt it."

"However it came, old man, you are correct," the Prince said. "It is the Hallow associated with Father Christmas."

"But why Father Christmas?" I blurted. "Father Christmas is...is...well, hang it, it's a Mystery for children!"

"It is more than that," said Colliston. "Father Christmas, or Santa Claus in America, is an ancient figure. It's one of the manifestations of the Mystery of Transformation."

"Transformation?" I asked.

"Think of it, Arthur," Winston said. "At this time of year, winter is transformed into spring and darkness into light."

"And selfishness into giving," Colliston added. "Father Christmas is a Mystery that can change and redeem the hardest heart. And yes, He *is* a children's Mystery, but children are the seeds of the future. They transform our present into the future. He guards their innocence and wonder. His Mystery is the magic of giving, hope, and joy that makes this a season of charity, a time of opening to the Light."

"And with the Hallow missing?" I asked. "What is the consequence? Surely people will not stop giving or celebrating Christmas or opening to Light."

"I fear that is exactly what may happen," His Royal Highness said. "Without the Hallow being present, the Mystery cannot touch the earth or walk amongst us, giving His blessings. Without the magic of this Being flowing through the world at this time of year, people may be disheartened by the coldness and strictures of winter. They may turn inward, into themselves, away from others, huddling over the fires of their own needs, their own survival."

"Surely not!" I exclaimed. "Giving and joy are human qualities, not bound to some magical entity however powerful it may be."

Colliston sighed. "Would that you were right. In time this will be true. The Hallows are seeds, as I said, whose power will grow within humanity until all Humanity itself is a Hallow. But we have not reached that time as a species, I fear. We still need models, inspiration, help from the Great Ones. That is why we have the Mysteries in our midst. And the problem is even direr. For the Hallows are threads interwoven through the world. Remove one and the whole skein may come unraveled, like the loose thread that undoes a sweater."

"And besides," added Winston. "Think of hundreds of thousands of disappointed children if the Mystery doesn't show up on Christmas Eve to bless their homes and spread his magic."

"Then what is to be done?" I exclaimed.

"The answer is obvious," replied Winston. "We must go to Mars. That is where the Hallow is, ergo that is where we must be if we are to bring this to a successful conclusion."

I shuddered. I do not mind telling you that in those days, I had become something of a homebody. My dear wife had died, my children had grown, and I had become comfortable living with Winston and helping him in his adventures. I didn't mind gallivanting around the globe, but the idea of hurling myself millions of miles into space to another, alien world.... I did not relish the thought.

But Winston seemed positively afire, his eyes gleaming with excitement. He turned to Colliston. "The deleterious effects upon Christmas and humanity due to the loss of this Hallow, will they happen immediately?"

"I cannot say for sure. There is a momentum built up from previous years that may carry us through, but I fear that as the Day approaches, the loss of the presence of Father Christmas will be felt in many ways. And other Hallows may be weakened as well."

"Then there is no time to waste," Winston exclaimed. He faced the Prince. "Sire, forgive my boldness in offering advice, but you and the Palace must do all in your power to promote the spirit of the Season. It may well be that your example and that of our Sovereign, your mother, will make up for what we have lost, at least for this year." He turned to me. "And Arthur, you and I, if you are willing, old friend, must embark for the Red Planet immediately! Christmas is next week!"

"Then our cause is doomed," said the Prince. "My personal ether craft is at your disposal, of course, but even at its top speed, it will take a week to reach that benighted world."

"I believe the Inner Lodge may be of assistance here," Colliston said. "There are other ways to travel that are faster, but there are risks..."

"Angelic apportation, much as you used to bring us to this chamber earlier," Winston said.

"Quite so, although I used my own small power to bring us here. To travel to Mars we shall need the invocation and help of one of the solar angels. This is no small matter. The journey will be instantaneous, but you will be in close proximity to one of God's Messengers. Only the truly pure in heart can hope to survive such an encounter."

"In this cause, it is a risk I must take. I do not hold myself a saint, but I do not fear for my soul. I must do what I must," Winston said. I believed him. If ever there were a modern Lancelot, pure and noble in all ways, it was my friend. Even more so, for he had no Guinevere to lust after, nor would he even if she existed, so disciplined were his mind and will. I, on the other hand, was another matter. Not that I am a sinful man, you understand, but I do not hold myself as being on as lofty a plane as Winston. My soul has integrity, but I imagine it has its stains as well.

"Well said, old man!" exclaimed the Prince.

"Yes, well said," agreed Colliston. He turned to me. "I sense some trepidation in you, but let me reassure you, you are a good man. I can see your aura and feel the vibration of your soul. You have naught to fear either."

I bowed to him, a sense of relief and gratitude swelling in my breast. "I thank you, Sir. Your words give me great comfort and confidence."

"Then let us be about this immediately," said Winston. "I see no reason to delay."

"It will take me a few moments to prepare," said Colliston. "I must journey from my body and contact one of the solar angels and petition its help. I am sure in this hour of our need, we will not be refused, but it will take me time. In the meantime, compose yourselves." He went into the center of the room and sat cross-legged on the floor after the manner of a Hindoo fakir. Closing his eyes, he went into meditation. I could feel a cone of silence and peace descend around him.

The three of us backed away and sat with our backs against one of the walls of the room, awaiting the arrival of the angel. As we sat, I turned to my companions and whispered, "I still do not understand why the Martians have done this. Of what use is Father

Christmas to them? In this place, are there not more powerful Hallows they could have taken, ones that could strike to the very Sovereignty and Power of the Empire? Why choose that one?"

"Perhaps the thief did intend to steal more but was limited in time," replied the Prince. "Perhaps he just chose at random."

"I cannot say," said Winston. "That knowledge was not vouchsafed me, either by my own powers of reason or by inspiration. Speculation is useless. The reason is what we must uncover, and we shall not do so here in this chamber."

"I suspect, though," His Royal Highness continued, "that blackmail is the reason. The Martians resent our colonies on their planet. One cannot blame them, but dash it all, it is humanity's destiny to seek the stars. And their world has fallen into ruin. We do not come as conquerors but as saviors, bringing them the benefits of good British civilization to replace the one they lost. Frankly, I would expect gratitude, but they rebel against us. Holding a Hallow ransom gives them leverage to force our retreat. They could embarrass us and force the government to fall to a no confidence vote. It almost fell last week over the Mars issue."

"I think you've hit the nail on its head, your Highness," I replied. "Of course, that must be it! What do you think, Winston?"

"I can only repeat what I said. We do not know enough. It is a possibility, no more, no less, until we have more data. But I suspect more is involved."

"Really? But, Winston…"

My friend held up his hand. "Hush, Arthur. Something stirs."

And indeed, in the middle of the room, surrounding the sitting figure of the Master Adept of the Planetary Lodge, a light was growing. As if from a far distance, I could hear the faint sound of angelic presence approaching. Many people, all wiser and more poetic by far than I, have tried to describe that sound. The music of the spheres, they've called it. The Melody of Joy. A

Symphony of Splendor. The fact is there is no human equivalent for it. I'm not sure it's even a sound, though that is how our brains render it. I only know it is sweet beyond compare and stirs one to the depths. No one can hear it and remain unmoved, unchanged. I could feel my soul yearning within me, reaching out from me, and for a moment, I trembled with fear. People have been known to die in the presence of angels.

But all at once, even as a heavenly Grace was entering the chamber, something dark and discordant rose in our midst. The music of the spheres turned to something alien, diabolical and soul-rending, the cry of souls in torment. The room seemed suddenly cold and empty as if it had opened to the eternal dark between the stars. Then a cloud of the most awful stench filled the air, and I began to choke, my eyes brimming with tears.

Beside me, Winston was on his feet, choking as I, but carrying something, a figure. I realized he had bodily snatched up the Prince and now was running to the door through which His Highness had originally come, bearing the royal heir to safety. "Get Colliston!" he ordered. "We have the devil in our midst!"

The thought of the Dark One storming our chamber filled me with horror. What had happened? The angelic presence had been so close. How could the forces of Hell enter this sacred room, with all its magical and mystical wards, even as a solar angel was entering as well? But then how had a thief entered? Perhaps this whole affair was really the work of diabolical forces masquerading as Martians. The Devil was, after all, the Father of Lies.

All these thoughts raced through my mind as, choking and weeping, I lurched forward into the dark cloud now emanating from the center of the room. By touch more than sight, for I was well-nigh blind, I found the Adept lying passed out on the floor. As Winston had done with the Prince, I slung this figure over my shoulder in a fireman's carry and staggered towards the door. Or where I thought the door was.

"This way, Arthur!" came Winston's welcome cry. I moved

toward the sound of his voice, and as I did so, the cloud lessened. I expected at any moment to feel demonic claws raking my back, but nothing of the sort happened. I came to the door and felt more than saw Winston's hand reach out from the corridor beyond and grip my arm. With a strong jerk, he pulled me through, and I collapsed on the floor of the corridor, Winston taking the burden of Colliston's body as I fell.

I lay there panting. The air was clear. Whatever had attacked us in the chamber of the Hallows did not reach into the corridor. And that itself was strange. What kind of force were we dealing with?

Winston was kneeling and administering to both the Prince and the Adept, drawing little vials of herbal concoctions of his own devising from his greatcoat's pockets. Soon, the two men had recovered and were sitting up, their faces streaked with tears.

"Good God," gasped the Prince weakly. "What was that?"

Colliston shook his head. "I have no idea. I have never encountered anything like that. I was returning in the company of the angel when I saw with inner vision something....something alien rise up in the room and strike, breaking my connection."

"Hell's own spawn, I warrant," I said, wiping my eyes with my handkerchief.

"No," said Winston. "I thought so, too, at first, but now I think not. This was not the devil's work, was it, Colliston? The Sovereignty of Britain resides in this room. Hell cannot prevail against it."

"That...that is correct."

"Besides, I have met Hell's own minions in the past, and this did not feel like them. It was alien. No, gentlemen, this was something else. A trap laid by our thief to prevent just the kind of angelic assistance as Colliston was summoning. It was cleverly triggered by the presence of the angel itself."

"But, Parnell, think what you're saying," the Prince said, his face clouded. "How could this be? The Martians are savages.

They're nomads living in the remains of a once-great culture. They have no science of this magnitude."

"This was no act of science, your Highness, but a magic most foul and powerful."

"But there are no Martian adepts, no field of magic there capable of this…is there, Colliston?"

The adept looked troubled. "What Parnell says is correct. I do not know what it is or how it happened, but we have been attacked by an alien magic of a kind I have never encountered. Yet, you also are correct, Sire. In the years we have been on Mars, there has been no trace of a Lodge there, no sign of adepts beyond tribal shaman, no unified planetary magical field or egrigore such as surrounds this world arising from the collected consciousness and work of adepts around the globe."

"Is it possible it is so alien as to be unrecognizable?"

"Possible, Parnell, but not likely. Magic works like science on universal principles."

"Well, this is getting us nowhere," I said. "Are we now blocked from invoking a solar angel? Cannot the room be cleared, and we try again?"

"A thorough cleansing will be necessary, indeed, but it will take time, time we do not have," replied Colliston. "And frankly, I am now weakened. The shock of being blasted back into my body has taken much from me, I'm afraid. It will take me time to recover."

"Then what are our options?" asked Winston. "We cannot be balked at the starting gate."

It was at that moment that a strange idea came to me. Where it came from, I do not know and hesitate to guess. I have always been a solid, dependable man, little given to flights of fancy, a scholar and a man of science. But at the same time, I am not unaware of the spiritual dimensions of life. While neither Lodgeman nor Churchman, I still have my devotions and appreciate, as the Bard himself once wrote, that "there are more things in heaven and earth than are dreamt of" in our philosophies. Indeed, I could hardly have associated with Winston Parnell for all these years and seen the things that we have seen without having that truth borne in upon me most forcefully.

So I did not question what happened next, and at the time, given the circumstances and the place where we were, it seemed almost ordinary. I was filled with an idea, no, more like a *persuasion*, a strong feeling that there was an action I needed to take. As I came to my feet, so the idea came full-blown into my consciousness. Without another thought, I ran back into the Chamber of the Hallows.

"Arthur!" cried Winston. "What th....?"

But I paid no attention. In that moment, a command from the Queen herself could not have drawn me back. The *persuasion* was upon me, a force so compelling and strong that I was obedient to it without question.

The room was still acrid with a sooty, reddish smoke, and my eyes immediately began to burn and weep again. But I paid them no mind. I ran to the display case where the Crown Jewels and the Regalia of Sovereignty lay in all their resplendence. As I did so, I removed my revolver from its place in my pocket and when I reached the case, I brought it down with great force upon the glass, which shattered with the blow.

Behind me I heard cries and exclamations from my companions, who, I sensed, were shocked into momentary paralysis by my strange and violent actions. They would come after me in a moment. But I cared not. I could *see* — I knew — what I must do. Knocking the pieces of glass aside, I dropped my revolver and reached into the case, removing the Sword of the Three Realms, known as the Jeweled Sword of Offering from the coronation of George IV, and the Sovereign's Orb surmounted by a jeweled cross. Turning, I held these up and cried out. I know not what words I used or the language they were in. It didn't matter. In that moment, clutched in the hands of fearsome inspiration, some very ancient part of me knew what to say and how to say it. I stood there, the Orb in my left hand, clutched to my heart, the Sword upraised in my right hand to the ceiling. I could see Winston, His Royal Highness the Prince of Wales, and the Master Adept, Colliston, all with stricken, unbelieving looks on their faces, rushing towards me, shouting, but I could not hear their words. The words I had spoken crashed and reverberated through my head, drowning out all else, and I felt a most terrible weight press down upon me, rooting me deep into the earth while another force seemed to stretch me out and out into the cosmos.

And then the room exploded.

Or so it seemed. There was a burst of Light, brighter than a thousand suns, and yet not hurtful in any way. Indeed, my own eyes stopped burning and weeping, and I felt like a young man in my prime, filled with vital energy and strength.

And in the center of the room, *She* stood.

How to describe Her? Was she fat or thin, blonde, redhead, or brunette, tall or short, a crone or a maiden? I cannot say.

She was the essence of grandeur, beauty, majesty, and love. Though her presence stood in the middle of the room, she seemed simultaneously to tower over all the land, holding us all in her calm and compassionate embrace. She was the Mother of all Goddesses, the Lady, the Soul of the World.

Out of the corner of my eye, I could see the three other men stop and fall to their knees in wonder and awe. But I couldn't move. I was rooted to the spot, holding the Orb, the Sword stretched above my head. She looked at me and smiled, and I would have gladly given my life a thousand times over for the grace and benediction of that smile.

She walked over to me. "Thank you for summoning me. Like your namesake, the ancient blood of this land sings in you and calls me forth. You stand in the lineage of the Grailseekers." Then She took the Orb and the Sword from my hands, and it felt as if a great weight was lifted from me. Gently She laid them back in the display case. A wave of Her hand and all was as it was, the glass restored to wholeness. I could feel the weight of my revolver restored to my pocket.

She walked over and touched each of the other men in turn, drawing him to his feet. The Prince She kissed on the forehead, saying, "Soon this head will wear the Crown. Serve my people and the land well."

The Prince straightened and I could truly see the Light of Kings in his eyes. "I shall, My Lady. Never fear."

She then held Colliston's hands, "Hail to thee, Master and Hierophant of the Inner Lodge. Tend the Light in my world."

"It is my undying honor to do so, my Lady," he replied.

She came to my friend, Winston Parnell. "My champion," was all she said, and he bowed his head. A flame appeared in the air beside her. She reached into it and pulled forth a sword. It blazed in the Light that emanated from her, and I could see the hilt was intricately carved with symbols and shapes I did not recognize. She handed it to Winston, who took it solemnly in his outstretched hands. "Save a world," She said.

"By my honor, Madam," he replied.

"I send you now to my Sister," She said, "but take care. All is not what it seems."

With that she beckoned me forward to stand beside Winston. She laid her hands upon our heads in benediction, and there was another flash of light. Our eyes were dazzled, and when we could see again, we were high on the slope of a bluff looking out over a vast desert plain the color of dried blood. The sun was high in the sky but smaller than normal.

"My God, Winston! Where are we?" I took a breath. The air was breathable but thin. And though the sun was overhead, it was cold. I shivered.

"Mars, I would say, my dear fellow. It seems angels are not the only way to travel!"

Winston was still carrying in his hands the sword he had been given, but now I saw a scabbard strapped around his waist. "It would seem the Lady expects us to run into trouble," I said.

"No doubt," my friend replied. "But remember her last words. 'All is not what it seems.'"

"What the devil does that mean?"

"I don't know, but I think we may be about to find out." He pointed off to the left, where a cloud of dust indicated riders headed our way. He sheathed his sword. "I doubt they are enemies, though. Their arrival is too propitious to be anything other than a result of our Lady's intervention."

I shivered again, beating my arms together. "Then if they are friends, let us hope they have blankets. And oxygen bottles would be good!"

"Come, my friend," he said, "it's no worse than when we were fighting the Yeti in the Himalayas. You'll get used to it quick enough, I warrant." He fixed me with a glare. "Arthur, enlighten me. Whatever possessed you to do what you did back on earth, seizing the Orb and Sword the way you did? My dear fellow, I thought you'd taken leave of your senses."

"I suppose I had. I have no idea. Perhaps it was the Lady herself, or the influence of the Hallows. It suddenly came over me that that was what I had to do."

"Well, it was jolly good you did. We were well and truly balked back there, with Colliston out of action that way."

"I'm sure His Highness thought I'd become a lunatic, or worse, an anarchist."

Winston chuckled, his gaze now on the fast-approaching riders. "I daresay. Had you seized the Crown instead and placed it on your head, there would truly have been hell to pay!"

The riders came closer, and soon we could see three figures riding on the strangely undulating six-legged beasts that were the common mounts for the blue-skinned nomads of Mars. They had two extra beasts in tow, obviously for Winston and myself. Save for the extra pair of legs, they resembled nothing so much as giant deer, sporting impressive antlers, until one opened its jaws and I could see rows of dagger-like teeth. I was suddenly glad for the revolver whose reassuring presence I could still feel in my pocket.

The riders were clothed head to foot in robes the color of the desert around us, looking much like the Bedouin on earth. Even their eyes were covered with goggles of strange design, no doubt to protect them from the blowing dust as they rode. Two of them were of human stature, but the third was obviously a drone, sitting tall and broad upon the largest of the beasts.

Without a word, one reached into a pack behind him and withdrew two robes similar to the ones they wore. He threw them at us and made it obvious by signs that we were to don them. I did so quite gratefully, for the cold was truly settling into my bones. With these robes about us, he handed us goggles which we also put on, then pulled the hoods over our heads. He reached into his pack once more and this time handed each of us a handful of grey leaves looking like nothing so much as seaweed. He made eating motions. I looked at Winston doubtfully.

"It's all right, Arthur. This is *marf*, a plant that grows ubiquitously on this planet. I have read several monographs about its remarkable properties. It will help your body metabolize the oxygen in the air more efficiently, making breathing easier." He immediately popped his handful in his mouth and began chewing.

Dubiously, I followed his example, remembering as I did so my son writing me about this stuff in one of his letters. Apparently, all the natives ate it, and now the troops did as well. Surprisingly, it was sweet and pleasant to the taste, reminding me of nothing so much as honey and cinnamon with a hint of orange.

Our allies then brought forward the two extra mounts. Carefully, Winston and I climbed onto the elaborately carved saddles on their backs. Then, once settled, the leader gave a whistle and we all trotted off towards the top of the bluff.

We moved swiftly, the dust billowing around us as we went. I was very glad for the hood that protected my face and the goggles for my eyes. I would have wished for a softer saddle, however. And while these beasts, known in the native tongue as *koraks*, might look like deer, they ran like sea-sick camels, undulating along on their six legs. For a time, I wondered if my recently eaten *marf* and I might violently part company as waves of nausea assaulted me. But in time, my stomach settled down, my breathing improved, and I began to feel fit once more.

We had obviously arrived in foothills at the base of a great mountain and our destination was somewhere amidst the higher crags and peaks. Shadows were lengthening as the sun dipped lower in the sky as we made our way, more slowly now as the terrain had grown more rugged, down what seemed a dry riverbed. Around us towered mountainous crags and cliffs hundreds of feet high. We were evidently in the Northern Highlands where the K'Thar clan predominated

Winston brought his *korak* close to mine and pointed to the ground beneath us. "It's an ancient road, Arthur," he said. "Here and there I have noticed signs of artificial construction. We may be en route to one of the ruins that dot this world."

I looked about, but no such signs made themselves evident to me, and I wondered just what Winston's keen senses had picked out from the general desolation around us. But at that moment we rounded the corner of a bluff and my friend's deductions proved correct once again.

On either side of the path we were following—the ancient roadway, according to my friend—two statues reared up some twenty feet, each depicting a humanoid warrior with a raised and outthrust weapon resembling a pike. These crossed over the roadway so that we rode under the weapons as if under a ceremonial archway. And ahead of us was a sight that took my breath away. Carved into the very face of the mountainside was a city of blackest stone.

My son had written me of the cliff cities of Mars, nearly all of which are in ruin now. They resemble some of the cliff towns of northern Africa or the dwellings of the Anazazi of the North American Southwest, but they are much more elaborate. Towers, minarets, flying buttresses, cathedrals, domes, great balconies, spiraling walkways, all thrust out from the mountainside. And here and there were other great statues, some of warriors, others of robed figures, some obviously feminine.

We rode along what became more and more clearly a roadway towards this mammoth city. It seemed perfectly preserved to me, not a ruin at all. But it was empty. Nowhere along its many walkways or windows did I spy a single figure. It was as dead as the rock from which it was carved.

Ahead of us a wall thrust out from the city itself, curving in a great semicircle out from the cliff face. In it a great portal at least thirty feet in height opened, obviously leading into an inner courtyard that was anteroom to the city itself, and towards it we rode. But just before passing through it, the leader gave a shrill whistle and led us off to the right. We paralleled the wall to our left until we came to a small corral built of stone just outside the great wall. Here other figures were standing, all clothed in dark red robes that covered them completely, obviously waiting for us.

As we approached, they opened a gate into the corral and we rode in, our beasts obviously recognizing this place as home. Troughs with food and water lined the sides of the corral, and the koraks were eager to get to them. Standing by the railing of the corral, we saw three drones, each at least nine feet tall, unrobed, wearing only leather harnesses and loin cloths, seemingly indifferent to the cold, the muscles of their four arms bulging. They looked formidable indeed, and their small, cold eyes watched our every move.

We halted, and the other robed figures ran forward and helped us dismount. In all this, not a word was spoken. The figure who had been the leader of our party came up to us and with hand signs indicated we should follow him. We did so, taking off our goggles as we went. I started to undo my hood to let it fall back so I could see better what was around me, but I was stopped by one of the Martians near me who indicted I should keep it on. I shrugged and did so.

We were led towards a smaller doorway in the great wall. Passing through it, we entered an open space divided into smaller walls no higher than my shoulder that ran in a zig-zagged fashion throughout the courtyard, effectively turning it into a kind of maze. I realized that should enemy soldiers breach the wall, they would be unable to run directly to the city but would be channeled through these many passages and mazeways open to fire from the defenders above.

The Martian leading our party, however, knew exactly how to twist and turn through the maze, and we were soon before a portal that led into the darkness of the city carved into the mountain above us. The way inward was lit by torches. As we passed into the city proper, we were enveloped in silence. This was truly, I felt, a city of the dead.

The walls of the corridor on either side of us were carved with ingenious designs and glyphs, all meaningless to me but attractive to the eye nonetheless. Occasionally a frieze came into view with figures in different stages of actions, the whole apparently narrating some ancient tale. When these appeared, Winston immediately went to them and began studying them, only to be nudged along gently but insistently by our escorts.

A five-minute walk brought us into a vast, open space the summit of which disappeared into the gloom. Buildings toward above us, both freestanding and carved into the cave walls themselves. All of them were dark save for one circular, two-story edifice directly ahead of us. It was ablaze with interior candlelight and torch light. It was to that place that our escorts directed us.

Inside, we found ourselves in a central chamber from which smaller rooms exited like bumps around the rim of a wheel. In the center of the room was a shining globe that gave off heat and light, though through what means I could not tell. Apparently, the Martians did have some technology at their disposal.

On one side of this globe were scattered large cushions and divans in what was obviously arranged as a sitting room. On another side of the globe was a place for dining, with a long table easily able to seat a dozen or more, with wooden chairs drawn up to it. Seeing it reminded me that aside from the *marf*, I had not eaten since dinner that evening on earth, however many hours that was ago, and I suddenly felt ravenous. Winston, as usual, seemed wholly unbothered by the needs of his body and upon entering the room had begun studying the central globe intently.

"Amazing, Arthur," he said, touching the artifact. "This is cool to the touch and feels like marble, but it radiates heat."

I might have responded with some agreement of astonishment, but at that moment, my attention was directed to a figure coming out from one of the smaller rooms. To my surprise, it was a human woman and a most comely one at that with shimmering blonde hair that reached to her shoulders. She was dressed in an explorer's outfit with dark trousers of a rough material and a khaki jacket with multiple pockets, which did nothing to hide her femininity.

"I say…." I muttered.

"Greetings, gentlemen," she said, and her voice was husky and melodic with a trace of accent that I could not place but which, I had no doubt, Winston would identify with ease.

"Madam," I said, giving a slight bow in her direction.

"Ah," said Winston, turning to face her. "You are the Lodge Priestess, and an archeologist to boot, unless I miss my guess."

She looked startled, then laughed, a most delightful sound, I had to admit. "And how have you come to those conclusions?"

"Elementary, Madam," he replied. "As for being an archeologist, you carry the tools of your trade in the bottom left pocket of your jacket there." Glancing where Winston had indicated, I saw the tips of a small brush and tiny trowel sticking up, both implements used for fine work in uncovering some buried artifact. "There are not many women on Mars as yet, and those who are present are mainly following scholarly professions, of which archeology is primary as the Martian ruins are studied. It takes no leap of imagination to see that this city is a major find worthy of such study."

"Well done, Mr. Parnell," she replied. With a sweep of her hand, she indicated we should sit on the couches or divans before us. "And as for being a Priestess?" she asked as she sat herself.

"You obviously know who we are and have been expecting us. You evidenced no surprise when we entered. When we were apported here, there was every indication from the Great One who effected our transport that our coming would be anticipated or at least announced. But to whom would such an announcement be made? Who would have the requisite abilities to receive either telepathic or mystical transmissions across time and space but someone trained and disciplined in the Lodge knowledge of a high degree. Such a person would almost certainly be an initiate, and seeing a woman before me, I conclude you are such an initiate and thus a Priestess or Sybil."

"Ah, but I could just be an archeologist, as you say, informed by such an initiate of your coming but not one myself."

Winston nodded. "Yes, that is true. But, and here is where I am in waters as yet uncharted by me and a bit troubling, some part of me senses there is more about you than that. You have an…." he struggled for a moment for the right word or concept, something I rarely saw my friend ever do, "an *aura* about you that says you are more than what you seem on the surface, that deep powers lurk within your soul. It pains me to recount such ineffable and….intuitive…perceptions, as they are quite new to me, but if they come from an inner sense like any other, I must learn to include it in my deliberations as I would the information from my eyes or ears."

"Then let me reassure you, Mr. Parnell, that you are quite

correct. I am Julia Edwards, a Lodge Priestess and a Doctor of Archeology from the University of Glasgow. As you have deduced, I was informed of your coming and that of your associate, Mr. Matthews. And as a Lodgewoman, I am glad you are admitting intuition into your armarium of intellectual talents."

"Thank you. But my skills are not the question here. If you were informed of us, you must equally have been informed of our need and purpose. We seek the Hallow that was stolen from the Earth. Do you know its whereabouts? Time is of the essence."

She frowned. "What do you know of Mars, Mr. Parnell, and of the Martians? Of their politics or their customs and organization?"

"Hear now!" I exclaimed. "Did you not hear Winston say time is of the essence? I hardly think this is a moment for discussing Martian politics and sociology, Madam."

But Winston held up his hand indicating I should be silent, as he replied, "I know some, Madam, based on what I have read. Is there specific information you feel I should have that bears upon our present situation? For my colleague is right, we have little time for intellectual discourse however pleasant and stimulating that might be under other circumstances."

"You're quite right. But most earth people see Martians either as savages or as the remnants of a lost civilization currently without power or culture of their own. To some extent this is true. Much has been lost. But these are neither ignorant nor powerless people, as the very theft of the Hallow itself proves."

"Such a theft would indicate a powerful science unknown to humanity," Winston said, "or an equally powerful magic. No indications of either have ever been found on Mars, though if this globe is an indication, we perhaps have not been looking hard enough or in the right places."

"Oh, there's technology here, Mr. Parnell. I've found evidence of that myself, such as this heater whose principles of operation are as yet undetectable. But it is ancient technology and most of it is not functioning. Still, it shows these were a proud and cultured people at one time, and that pride exists today. They do not take lightly to being a conquered people."

"Hardly conquered, Madam," I interjected. "We are colonizing this world, yes, but there is room enough for everyone. We have not taken anything from the natives save perhaps a life doomed to ignorance, squalor, and degradation."

I thought I saw a trace of annoyance as she looked at me. Was she, perhaps, one of those whose involvement with the peoples they study took them beyond the bounds of objective and rational observation, to where they become so identified with their subjects that they end up going native? "There are those who would disagree with you, Mr. Matthews. And violently so. They see you as infidels sullying a sacred land and would be rid of you all."

"You say "you" rather than "us," Madam, as if you do not count yourself a citizen of your own homeworld."

She smiled. "Ah but I do, Mr. Matthews, I do. But it is my job to put myself into the minds and perspective of those long gone—the inhabitants of cities like this one—and inevitably it puts me into the minds of those now living."

"And in these living minds," Winston said, "we are invaders."

"Yes, for some. Not all. There are Martians who welcome the coming of the Terrans, for all the reasons you say, to bring the blessings of a new civilization. But there are others who resent it and would remove you from this world."

"And they would have the power to steal the Hallow."

"Apparently so, Mr. Parnell."

"But how? As Winston said, there is neither the technology nor the magic."

"As to the former, you are correct. As to the latter, I am not so sure."

"No adepts have ever been found," said Winston.

"Correction. No adepts have ever revealed themselves. This doesn't mean they don't exist. They may have chosen to remain in hiding to study their new adversary and determine an appropriate time to strike."

"I grant you your point, Madam," Winston replied. "But speculation gets us nowhere. The question to be answered is simple. There is a reason the Lady of the World sent us here, to this place. And that you were summoned to help us. It is not mere happenstance. Either you know something we must know or the clue to the Hallow's whereabouts must be here, and here is where we must look."

An expression of doubt crossed the lady's face. "This is what troubles me. I was informed you were coming and why and asked to render you assistance, but that's all. I have no idea where the Hallow is. I have no idea why you were sent here…unless…."

"Yes, Madam? You suspect something?"

Instead of answering, she turned and called out something in a strange language. I assumed it must be Martian, for almost immediately one of the robed figures came into the room. They spoke swiftly to each other, the sound of the words melodic to my ear. It was the first I had heard the native tongue spoken, and it surprised me. For some reason, I had expected something less pleasing and cultured.

Winston, I could see, was beside himself with anticipation, straining to be on with it. Though with his towering intellect he lived a great deal in his mind, part of him was a man of action and adventure, not content to simply sit around and discuss when matters of consequence were at hand. He listened with fierce attention to the dialogue between Julia Edwards and the Martian, but his body was tense and ready to spring into action. I could see the fingers of his left hand caressing the hilt of the sword the Lady had given him, tracing over and over the strange designs carved thereupon.

The Martian bowed to the Lodge Priestess and turned,

running out of the room. Julia Edwards turned back to us. "These cities are not entirely dead, gentlemen. They still provide refuge for groups of Martians. But most Martians are superstitious. They do not come to these cities for fear of angering the ancestors. So, most cities are abandoned, like this one. But recently, my men have seen small groups of nomads making their way to the northernmost end of the city. It may mean nothing, but it is unusual."

"But it may mean some congregation is occurring. It bears investigating." Winston sprang to his feet. "Can you show us where these nomads are gathering? We must make our way there immediately."

She hesitated. "It would be dangerous. The K'Thar clan rules these hills, and they have factions that despise Terrans. They would kill you if you are discovered and likely torture you first. It is why we all go fully robed and covered when outside these walls. I do not want to advertise the fact that those other than natives are present." I remembered that one of our escorts had stopped me from pulling back the cowl of my robe.

She shuddered. "I have seen carvings that make my blood run cold. The ancient Martians devised intricate ways to torture their prisoners and boasted about it in stone on their walls. Their descendants may be no less inventive."

"It is no matter, Dr. Edwards. This matter must be dealt with and the Hallow restored. We shall simply trust courage and spirit to see us through."

"My man says there were many drones among the nomads. It may be a warrior clan you face."

"As Winston said, stout British heart and strength of arm have rarely failed," I assured her. "Have faith and we shall prevail."

She smiled. "Then I shall send one of my men to show the way. Unfortunately, most of them do not possess your courage—or foolhardiness—and run if confronted with warrior drones. It would be useless to send them, but Tilian is the bravest of the lot and will guide you true."

"We are grateful," Winston said.

"And of course, I shall be with you."

Before I could protest, Winston held up his hand and said, "No, Dr. Edwards, this cannot be. And wait, before you protest, I say this not because of your fair sex. I know that the path to becoming a Lodge Priestess demands the highest moral and physical courage. I have no doubt your presence would be an asset, but we need you here. You are our only link with Earth and the Planetary Lodge should something go amiss. If Arthur and I do not return, you must be safe to put out the word that other means must be found to rescue the Hallow."

"I see. Yes, of course, you are right. But the two of you against a warrior clan!"

"You forget we have the advantage of gravity. To the Martians, we are superhuman in our strength. And I have a good blade as well." Winston drew his sword, and its blade gleamed almost as if gave off light rather than merely reflecting it from the surrounding torches.

Seeing it, the Priestess drew back, her face suddenly pale. "That...that sword! Where did you get it?"

"Why, the Lady herself gave it to Winston," I exclaimed. "'Save a world' is what she said, and 'tis what we'll do."

"Are you all right, Dr.Edwards," asked Winston, sheathing his blade and stepping forward to take her arm in support. "You look faint."

"It...it is a puissant blade indeed," she said, stepping back and taking a deep breath. I could see her composing herself. "I had not expected to see it here or to feel its power. I was merely taken by surprise when I felt its force. You are indeed well-armed, Sir." She turned and shouted, and two of the natives came in. Again, a liquid trill of sentences followed. One of the Martians ran off, but the other came forward and bowed. "I Tilian. Lead you, shall I," he said in halting English.

"He speaks our language?" Winston asked.

"A little bit. I found it easier to learn their tongue than to teach them ours. But he will understand your commands and will have some ability to communicate with you."

"Excellent!" said Winston. "Then we must be off."

We followed Tilian out of the room. I saw Winston look back, and a frown crossed his features. Glancing back myself, I saw Dr. Edwards straining to push open a door carved into the wall of the room. It resisted her efforts at first, and then swung inward revealing a torchlit passageway, obviously to another part of the house. But then she was lost to view, and Winston and I were hurrying to catch up with our guide.

He took us first to a table where various packages were stacked. Opening one, he took out a handful of wrapped bars and handed three to each of us. He made eating motions. "Eat. Food." he said.

I gratefully unwrapped one of the bars and took a bite. It was delicious. I recognized the flavor of *marf* and something else. "Very nice," I said, wolfing it down and opening a second.

"Come. Eat and walk," he said.

He led us through abandoned corridors and passageways, down stairways and up ramps until I was thoroughly lost. We were obviously heading deeper into the city. At one point, Winston stopped him and said, "We must go through the city?"

"Safer," Tilian said, nodding his head up and down. "Cutting small."

"You mean, it's a shortcut?"

"Yes." More head nodding. "Short...cut. Yes. Come!"

We continued on. Our way was fitfully lit by torches set at regular intervals into the walls of buildings and at times into the mountain side itself. In some places, tall poles held globes that emitted a pale light and warmth, further evidence of an unknown technology. But mostly it was a journey through shifting shadows that disoriented my vision and left me feeling totally lost as to where we were or the direction in which we were headed.

At one point, we passed one of the friezes. It was long, running for a whole city block and telling some intricate story which looked to me like a group of robbers making off with stolen goods. Many of the figures carried bulging sacks or were holding sacks up to the sky. At one point, I saw a figure that I thought I recognized. It was damnably familiar, but I didn't know how or why. Had we not been in such a hurry, I would have lingered to look more closely and puzzle the thing out. But we rushed on, and soon the sculptures disappeared into the shadows behind us.

Eventually we came to a place where there were no more torches. Tilian reached into his robe and came out with three long sticks, each about two feet in length, two of which he passed to us. He shook his violently and it suddenly burst into a cold, bluish light. "You...shake stick," he said. Winston and I did as he had done, and our sticks also came alight. But there was no warmth from the stick.

"Hmmn," muttered Winston, examining his stick, "cold fire. Obviously, a chemical reaction of some sort. Perhaps sodium and ammonium cabonate, luminol, hydrogen peroxide, and copper sulfate pentahydrate...chemicals are kept separate until the shaking breaks their seal and mixes them, causing this reaction...."

The man's encyclopedic knowledge always astounded me.

We plunged on in a darkness banished only by the light from our light sticks. I could feel the dark presence of stone buildings all around me. But then, all at once, I knew we had entered a courtyard or public square of some nature. I felt the space around me widen on all sides, and the sound of our footsteps changed, echoing into the distance. I held up my light stick. Vaguely I could see tall hulking forms around us. I peered closely at one and saw it was a statue of a drone, a huge battleaxe clutched in two of its hands, a shield and sword in the other two. Not someone I wanted to meet on a battlefield!

And then the statue moved.

"Winston!"

"I see them! It's an ambush."

I heard footsteps and saw Tilian running for his life back in the direction we had come. So much for his standing with us in the face of danger.

In the dark I could not see how many of the brutes there were. There could be hundreds in the vast unknown space before us, in which case we were truly undone. I knew our only chance was to back up into the crowded passageways between the buildings where the drones could not surround us but had to come at us one at a time.

Winston, however, had other ideas.

He whipped out his blade which blazed with holy fire in the darkness. It was brighter than the light stick he held in his left hand, and in its glow, I could see about a dozen of the drones advancing on us, all of them nine feet tall or taller. With a shout, Winston leaped forward, bringing his blade down upon the nearest of the creatures. To my amazement, he cleaved the brute from crown to the middle of its chest, then sprang back as blue blood spurted upward from the fatal blow. The drone collapsed with a crash, dropping its battleaxe and sword. Winston waved his sword at the others and charged between the next two closest. They silently swung their battleaxes at him and jabbed with their swords, and I knew that if either weapon connected, my friend would be cleaved in half or skewered like an Arab's *shish kabob*. But Winston moved with a fluid grace born of years of practice of qe-wan do and other exotic martial arts from the mystical East. The blades of the drones missed him by inches, but the swing of his blade did not, and two more of our opponents fell before him.

The rest of the horde stopped, unsure what to do, suddenly unwilling to come within reach of his glowing, deadly blade.

This had all happened so swiftly that I had simply stood there, gaping. My wits returned with a crash. I reached beneath the robes and pulled out my faithful Webley. I aimed in the direction of one of the drones and fired twice. I must admit that I am a crack shot, and the bullets hit the Martian square in the chest. It staggered back, but otherwise showed no effect. I aimed again, and this time caught it square between the eyes. The drone collapsed with a sigh, his weapons clanging to the rock floor around him.

"Good shot, old man!" Winston cried. "Think you can do it again?" And with that he bellowed and hurled himself at two others of the brutes, his sword raised like wrath itself above his head.

"Of course," I yelled back, and I did. Another drone fell, and then two others, dispatched by Winston's blade and prowess.

At this point, the other drones turned and vanished into the darkness.

Not winded at all, Winston came back to stand by me. "That was well done," he said, wiping his blade on his robe and sheathing it.

"Good God, man, what possessed you to attack them? They were monstrous!"

"They were warriors, Arthur, and warriors respect courage. I knew if we retreated, it would embolden, even enrage them, and they would follow. By attacking I proved we were unafraid and formidable. And remember, on this world we are super strong. They were no match for me or this blade. Or for your shooting. Excellent marksmanship, old friend, and in such poor lighting, too!"

He bent down and examined the warriors. I leaned over him. "Our guide has been frightened off. What shall we do now?"

"Why, we head back to where we started, to where Dr. Edwards is."

"To get another guide?"

"No. We don't need another guide."

"But Winston, I don't know if I could even find my way back to our starting point, much less press onwards without a guide."

"We don't need to press onwards. The Hallow is not in front

of us. It's behind us."

"What? Why do you say that? How can that be?"

"Look, Arthur. Look at the leather harnesses on these drones. Do they look familiar?"

I looked at the harness, but I could not see anything out of the ordinary about them. "I don't know. One harness looks like another."

"Ah, but they don't, my friend. At least, not between one clan and another. When we arrived at the corral, do you remember the drones we saw standing there?"

"Yes, I...Good God, man! Are these them?"

"Them or their clan brothers. I recognize the harness markings. These drones are not from the encampment ahead of us, assuming there is one. They're from behind us. That was no shortcut Tilian took us on. I have an unerring sense of direction, even underground, as you know. He was taking us on a circuitous route to give these drones time to get into place for the ambush."

"But that means.... My God, Winston, they must have taken Dr. Edwards captive!"

"Calm yourself, my friend. She is most certainly not a captive. She is the one behind this plot."

I looked at my friend, his face eerily illumined by our light sticks to see if he were kidding me, but he was deadly serious.

"Explain yourself."

He stood up and brushed himself off. "Let us head back. We have very little time, I'm afraid. I'll tell you my reasoning as we go."

I looked back through the darkness at the passageway from which we had come. "Do you know the way back?"

He chuckled. "Like I said, I have an unerring sense of direction. It's not possible to get me lost. You should know that by now, old friend." And in fact, I did. So, I fell into line with him, and we started back through the city.

"The clues have been right there before me," he said. "What have we been saying all along? The Martians have neither the technology nor the adepts to accomplish such a feat as the stealing of the Hallow. So, who does?"

"I don't know, Winston. Who?"

"Why, we do, of course. Not you and I, of course, but the Empire. We have the technology and we have the adepts."

"We've stolen the Hallow from ourselves? Winston, that doesn't make sense."

"Ah, but it makes perfect sense, Arthur. I do not know the details, of course, but I will. But remember what Dr. Edwards said about the politics among the Martian factions?"

"Yes."

"It isn't just the Martians that are divided over the colonization program. There is a strong Leave Mars to the Martians faction in our parliament as well. Millions of pounds Sterling are being spent to maintain our troops on this planet to protect our holdings and so far without a lot to show for it. The colonies are struggling. The government almost fell last week, you may recall, on a confidence vote. If for some reason, the Martians could embarrass the government and even blackmail it, I have no doubt the current administration would fall."

"That's what the Prince feared as well. He said as much."

"He's right. But what if it's not a Martian faction but an earth faction, one with Lodge support? A powerful group of Lodge adepts could conceivably do what has been done. And remember what the Lady said: 'All is not what it seems.'" We may be facing a domestic plot, not an interplanetary one."

"The loss of Christmas would be a blow no government could sustain. Why, it could even affect the Palace."

"Indeed, Arthur. This, I think, is why this Hallow was chosen. The others represent abstract forces for the average man, but the loss of Father Christmas, the sorrow of children, the darkening of the Holidays, that is something every person in the Empire, no matter how mean or humble, can understand. It would be a serious blow against the Crown. And it is a blow whose effects would be felt immediately. Coming on the heels of last week's vote, it could easily topple the government, perhaps even the Crown. I think we are on the trail of something more here than just the replacement of one government or another. There are those who have said the Crown is obsolete. The loss of the Hallow of Christmas could prove the Throne an unreliable guardian."

"Not that a President or Congress would do any better!" I exclaimed, thinking of those who longed to emulate our American allies and form a Republic. Ahead of us, I could see a glow of light. We were reaching the part of the city illuminated by torches and globes.

"I don't think that would come to pass. No, the logical replacement for the Crown would be the Adepts of the Lodges, a council of magicians."

"You're saying this is a plot of the Lodges against the Crown. Winston, that defies belief! The Lodges are one of the two pillars that support the Crown!"

"And history shows that pillars can crumble. I am not saying that all Lodgemen are in on this plot. I'm sure Colliston and the Planetary Lodge have no knowledge of it. But there is Lodge involvement, of that I'm sure. And as a Priestess, Dr. Edwards can tell us which Lodges they are."

I must confess that I was greatly troubled by what Winston had said. A Martian plot, no matter how nefarious or what alien powers it revealed, was infinitely preferable to me than the idea that one or more of our own Lodges and councils of Adepts could be involved in treason against the Throne. That turned my world upside down. Church and Lodge were supposed to be above politics. But I suppose where humans and power are concerned, nothing is beyond anything.

"There is one good thing about this, Arthur," Winston said as he thrust his light stick before him to negotiate a narrow passage between two buildings.

"For the life of me, I can't imagine what." I replied.

"It means the Hallow is safe."

"You mean it may not even be here on Mars?"

"Oh, no, it's on Mars. The Lady would not have sent us here if it were not. I can imagine no power on earth capable of suborning Her into being an accomplice to a human plot. But unless I'm wrong, one of the Lodges has it and will protect it from harm until their ends are met."

"Though that may destroy Christmas this year."

"Let us keep the faith, my friend. The Throne may yet supply the example that's needed to preserve the spirit of the Holiday. And I have not given up finding the Hallow. Indeed, once we confront Dr. Edwards, I do not believe it impossible we shall secure its release. But let us hurry. I'm not sure why, unless it's this damnable intuition I seem to have suddenly sprouted, but I feel our time is very limited indeed."

We rushed through abandoned streets until all at once we came to a place I recognized. It was the street with the frieze I had puzzled over, the one with the people carrying bags, and the figure I had thought I'd recognized. As Winston rushed forward, intent upon returning to the round house at the entrance to the city, I paused just a moment to look again at the figure that had tantalized my imagination and my memory. Where on Mars could I have seen this before?

And then I remembered.

I hadn't seen it on Mars. I'd seen it in our study at home God knew how many hours earlier. I'd been reading a letter from my son. I reached under the robe and into my jacket pocket. Yes, the letter was still there where I'd folded it up and thrust it into my pocket. I quickly pulled it out and opened it. Looking at the sketch, I saw that it was indeed the same figure.

"Arthur," called Winston from up ahead. "This is not the time for sightseeing, old man!"

"Winston! Come see this. I know this figure." Looking at the rest of the frieze, I suddenly understood why the figures were carrying bags.

"Arthur, this is hardly the time," said Winston, coming up to me. I handed him the letter and pointed to the correspondence between the figure on the wall and the image my son had drawn. "Yes, it's a good likeness. But who is it?"

"It's Sulia, a Martian goddess. Once a year, she moves through the world collecting bags of woe from the people, particularly from children, thereby lifting them from depression and sadness and letting them wake up to joy."

"Your son wrote you this?"

"Yes. He was describing Martian children putting out these little bags—he called them 'woe-sacks'—once a year for Sulia to pick up and remove. The children here aren't given presents, but they have all the woes they've accumulated for the previous year taken away."

"And does She?"

"Does She what? Who?"

"Does Sulia take away the woe-sacks?"

"No. It's not like our Father Christmas who is a real being and does appear in homes each Christmas Eve to give a blessing—or does if the Hallow is there to permit it. Sulia is apparently just a legend. Maybe once there was such a being, but she long ago disappeared. Pity. Think of all the children left with their woes... I'm sure their parents dispose of the bags, though."

Winston looked down at the letter my son had written, and then back up at the figure on the frieze. Then he slowly walked along the wall examining the figures. Now it was my turn to become impatient. "Winston, I'm sorry I stopped us. You were right, we have to hurry. This isn't a time for sightseeing, just as you told me."

But he ignored me, and I could tell from the look on his face that he was suddenly deep in one of his deductive trances, humming his characteristic hum. There would be no rousing him until he decided to be roused. At one point, he ran his fingers over the figure of the goddess of Mars and the glyphs that surrounded her. And suddenly he shuddered and shook himself all over.

He whirled about and gripped my shoulders. "Arthur, I've been a fool. The evidence has been right before me all the time, and I ignored it. Worse, I jumped to wrong conclusions. My only excuse is that I've been put off my stride by these irrationalities and intuitions that have seized me lately. But now I know. I don't know everything yet, but I will. And I know that we truly must hurry, for in this regard my intuition was correct. We may only have a short time to save our world, if it is not already too late. Come, Arthur, run like the wind, or Earth may become the desolate twin of Mars."

With that he turned and began to run swiftly down the city street. Dumbfounded, I stood for a moment watching him, and then I took off after him. "Winston," I shouted. "What has come over you? What is happening?"

"You'll see soon enough," he shouted back. "Just pray we're not too late!" And as he ran, he tore off his robe so that it would not encumber his legs.

"Too late for what?" But this time there was no answer.

I will never forget that mad dash through the shadowed streets of this ancient, dead city of Mars, my robe flying back behind me until I, too, tore it off to keep up with my friend. Like fiends we ran, and it was as if all the gods of Mars chased us down those silent byways. Indeed, with our greater strength and in the lighter gravity, we ran like gods ourselves, making great bounds and leaps down the streets.

And then ahead was the round building where we had met Dr. Julia Edwards. As it came into sight, Winston stopped. I nearly slammed into him, and he grabbed my arm to steady me. "Caution now, Arthur. There may be more ambushes."

We moved forward towards the building, keeping as much

as possible to the shadows around us. As far as we could see, no one was about. Finally, we dashed across a small street and into the main room of the building. It was empty.

"Where the devil is everyone?" I muttered.

"Through here, I warrant," said Winston, rushing over to a carving in the wall. I remembered seeing Dr. Edwards pushing on it and going through into a lighted corridor. "Quiet now," he said, and pushed on the wall. The door opened before him, our greater strength making light work of its heavy construction. Before us lay the same lighted corridor, and coming up it, I could hear the sound of voices chanting.

"Have your revolver ready just in case, Arthur," he whispered, and obediently, I pulled the Webley from my pocket. Winston drew his sword.

With as much stealth as possible, we crept along the corridor and then down a winding flight of steps. Down and down we went, with the hypnotic sound of the chanting growing louder and louder.

We came out on balcony overlooking a vast amphitheater, brightly lit by hundreds of the radiant globes. I gasped. There were hundreds of blue Martians below us standing in a great circle around a dais on which stood an altar. Standing by the altar was Dr. Julia Edwards, but now she was garbed in a robe that appeared to be made of spun silver and gold and a blood red crown was atop her head. Around the base of the dais was a double circle of red robed figures.

The whole group was chanting, oblivious to everything but Dr. Edwards and the altar.

And on the altar was a wooden cup. The Hallow of Christmas.

I gasped at the scene below me.

"Winston," I whispered. "You were right. It's the traitorous Lodge below us."

Winston sighed with pleasure. "No, Arthur. I was wrong.

That is no Lodge, at least no earthly Lodge. Behold, the Adepts of Mars."

"Adepts of…but Winston, there are no Martian adepts. There is Dr. Edwards, the Lodgewoman and Priestess, and…."

"Arthur, believe me. These are the adepts of Mars. And that is not Dr. Edwards…or at least, Dr. Edwards is not what we thought."

"What do you mean?"

"I mean she's not human, Arthur. She's a Martian. And now we must stop one world from killing another. Look, they are entering into trance. Quick now, fire your revolver over their heads. We must stop this ritual before it's too late."

My head in a whirl from these new revelations, I did as Winston bade me. I fired three times over the heads of the mob below, and as the sounds reverberated through the chambers, the chanting stopped. At first there was confusion as the trance was broken, but then all heads turned to us, and I looked down upon hundreds of upraised, angry Martian faces.

I gulped. "Winston, if this is a Lodge, they can blast us where we stand."

"I think not," and he raised the sword above his head, its fiery light filling the cavern.

One of the red-robed Martians pointed at us. "Blast them," he shouted. Immediately I could feel a tremor in the air below us. Magical energy is subtle and easily unrecognized, but when it is massed in the presence of a Lodge it can take on tangible force. I could feel that force building, and then, suddenly, it was unleashed, rushing towards us as a shimmering wave of light. I caught my breath, knowing death was upon me.

But light hit light, the wave of force crashing into the light shimmering around the sword that Winston wielded, his own mighty will channeled through it to protect us. Like a wave breaking around us, I felt the force of the massed will of the adepts swirling around us and then dying down, even as the sword flared even more brightly.

Then a woman's voice rang like a clear bell through the chamber. "Stop! It is too late. They wield the Sword of Argath."

Suddenly it felt like all the energy swept out of the chamber, and a great wailing went up from the throats of the Martians below. Some collapsed, weeping upon the ground. I felt a depression, a sadness, come over me like none I had ever felt, and tears sprang to my eyes. It was as if we all wept for the death of a world.

Holding the sword before him, Winston descended the steps, and I followed, tears streaming down my cheeks, though I knew not why. The Martians parted before him as he made his way to the dais and then up to the altar. And there, tears in her eyes as well, the woman who had pretended to be Dr. Edwards stood before him. And changed.

Where a blonde human woman had stood, now a raven-haired, blue-skinned Martian woman looked at both of us, a stricken expression warring with a determination to present a proud face to the human interlopers.

Winston bowed to her. "The Priestess of Sulia, I presume."

"How do you know this?" she asked.

He shrugged. "You gave yourself away in small ways, but I did not have the wit to see them until it was almost too late." He turned to me. "Nor would I have seen them in time had it not been for you, old friend."

"Me? But Winston, what did I do?"

Rather than answer me, he turned back to the Priestess. "You were going to steal the power of the Hallow, weren't you? You were going to use the life of Father Christmas to revivify the goddess Sulia?"

She looked at us defiantly. "Not merely a goddess. The Lady of our world."

"Ah, of course." He nodded to himself. "'I send you to my Sister,' She said." He looked at the Priestess. "But why?"

"Why?" She laughed bitterly. "You have seen our world, and you ask why? Is our barrenness not reason enough? Is our helplessness before you not reason enough? Are not the crumbling ruins of our once-great cities not reason enough? Our children lay out their woe-sacks and no one takes them. No one can deliver us from our woes. Our children die from sadness. Our planet has become one great woe-sack. Where is Sulia to deliver us?" Tears began to fall from her eyes but she refused to acknowledge them.

"Where indeed?" Winston wondered. "What has happened to the Lady of your world? How could She have abandoned you?"

"She did not abandon us. She...was diminished."

"Diminished? What do you mean?"

"Drained of power and life. Bound to matter and mortal form."

Winston took a step back from her. "It's you, isn't it?"

She bowed her head, then looked up. "Yes. I am Sulia."

"My God," I said, "Our Lady really did send us to Her sister!"

"But how is this possible? You are an Immortal, one of the Mysteries of your world!" For once, Winston's incredible mind seemed to be struggling to understand.

"And I am immortal still. But for five thousand years I have been imprisoned in this city, bound by Argath, an Adept whose worship of power knew no bounds. He gathered a ring of the most powerful adepts of his day and constructed a ritual that split my power from me and channeled it into him and a Hallow he created. In the process, as he knew secretly would happen, the adepts were all killed and their power drawn into him as well. He sought to make himself one of the gods of Mars, and for a time he succeeded. But though he had power, he had no ability to sustain the life of this world, and our planet began to die. He refused to believe this, and in the madness of power he sought other worlds to conquer."

"Earth…" Winston said. "It would seem, Arthur, your Harvard professor may have been on to something."

"Yes, it was your world. But he failed in his attempt and never returned. And in the process, the Hallow that carried my power was lost with him."

Winston raised the sword in his hand. "And this is it, isn't it? You called it the Sword of Argath. There is a design carved into its hilt which I found also carved next to a picture of you in the city."

"Yes. It is a sigil that binds my power to the sword."

"Then if I give it to you, your power will be restored."

"If it were so simple, I would have asked you for it earlier when you first showed it to me. But it is cursed, at least to me. The adept bound his own power and life to it as well so that should I gain possession of it in some way and draw my power from it, I would draw him into me as well. I could not risk the chance that in my weakened state I might become corrupted. Truly, when he disappeared on your world, I never thought to see it again, and though I was diminished, I was glad. It is an evil thing."

"It was given to me by my Lady," Winston said. "It has been made pure."

"For you, perhaps. Not to me. I can feel the taint within it."

Winston sighed. "Then we are stalemated. Yet I have been charged to save this world. How can I do so?" He looked at the altar. "You have our Hallow. What were you going to do with it?"

"Siphon its power back into me in the hopes I would be restored. Of all the Mysteries in your world, the Mystery of your Father Christmas is most akin to my nature. Like him once a year I would visit my children and give them joy."

"By taking their woes from them."

"Yes. I would gather all their hurts and wounds, their pains and sorrows, their tears and sadness, and take them into my heart where they would be changed and healed and even turned into wisdom. And lightened from their burdens, their hearts would rise into joy, and perhaps touch the wisdom as well. But when my power was taken, I could no longer do that. So our woes gathered and gathered until we sank beneath them, and our greatness and our cities sank and crumbled, too, becoming what little you see today."

"But you survived."

"Of course. I am immortal. And I gathered the remaining adepts with me, those you see here, who had been pure and faithful, and I have kept them alive and protected as well, but only within this city."

"It was their power and magic that let you take this Hallow and prepared the trap for us on earth if we attempted to follow," I said.

"Yes."

"But where is Julia Edwards? Or was there never such a person?"

"She is safe and in our custody. I used her appearance to deceive you and send you on a fool's errand while we performed the ritual of transference. She is as I presented her, an archeologist and Priestess who came to this city and discovered me. She told me much about your world and about your Father Christmas. I could feel the kinship as she spoke. We are both Mysteries for children and for the promise of the future, a promise I have been unable to keep." She bowed her head for a moment in sadness, then looked up at us again defiantly. "You have such a rich world. You have everything we have lost. What would it matter if I drew one of your Mysteries to me and used it to give me life again?"

"Ah, Lady," Winston said, compassion in his voice, "you would know if you retained your power and could see the harm it would do. This Mystery is one of our most cherished and powerful. To lose it could unravel much. Our world could become as yours when your people lost you."

She paled. "I...I didn't realize... Perhaps I have been tainted by Argath's evil already."

"I think not," he said. "Only by unremitting years of sorrow and helplessness as your people diminished before your eyes."

"Winston," I asked, "How do you know all this? You thought it was a Lodge plot against the Throne."

Winston closed his eyes. "And I was wrong, almost fatally so." He looked at me and then back at Sulia. "I saw but did not at first recognize the clues. You spoke of this world as if it were your homeland. You recognized this sword and the power within it. You were here alone with no other earth men working with you in this city. No archeologist works without colleagues. I should have seen that immediately. Then I happened to see you struggle to open a heavy door when had you truly been a woman from earth as you claimed, your extra strength would have opened it with ease. Further, you stole a Hallow related to your own Mystery, to what you are. You even took an earth name like your own. So many clues. I was blind not to see them earlier." He sighed. "When you showed me the carving of Sulia, Arthur, in the city above and I saw the sigil there that is also on this sword, I began to wonder. Then I realized the link between Sulia and Father Christmas through children. That was when the scales fell away and I could see."

He frowned. "But now, I have gone as far as reason allows. I stand on a precipice, and before me is an abyss where intuition alone can go, an ally I have not needed but now require. I fear to take that step, for I sense it will change me irrevocably. But I have no choice. Save a world, my Lady asked. And save a world is what I must do."

He turned and lay the sword upon the altar. Carefully and gently he picked up the Hallow of Father Christmas, the Christmas Cup, and handed it to me. "Guard this with your life, Arthur."

"Winston," I said, trepidation rising in my chest, "what are you planning to do."

"Elementary, my dear fellow. If you had two liquids mixed and one were a poison contaminating the other and you wished to separate them, what would you do?"

"Why, I would distill them and let them separate, or I would pass them through a filter that held the one but passed the other."

"And that is what we shall do here, and I shall be the filter."

"Winston! No! You cannot do this!"

"I must. My…my intuition tells me this is what I must do." He turned to Sulia. "You must do your ritual, but now you must siphon the power from your own Hallow, now returned to you, through me. I shall endeavor to trap and hold the spirit of the ancient warlord and let what is of you pass into you."

"Winston, you cannot be serious," I exclaimed. "How can you trust her? If you haven't forgotten, she arranged an ambush and tried to kill us. She is an enemy!"

"No, Arthur, merely a desperate woman who once was much more and can be so again. In any event, I cannot refuse this test, for my own Lady has asked it of me."

"Can you do this?" Sulia asked, hope kindling in her eyes.

"My Lady thought I could. Therefore, I can!"

"But if you fail…Argath is an evil beyond compare. He could come to life in you."

"Then you must kill me straightaway, lest his evil work mischief through me. In that event, you will be no worse off than you are now. But if we succeed, and we shall, then you shall be restored and your world with you."

She looked at Winston, then nodded. "So let it be done."

"No!" I exclaimed. "I forbid it. If anyone is going to be a damn fool filter, it will jolly well be me! Remember, the Lady said I was a Grailseeker, that the blood of my namesake—that's *King* Arthur, Winston—runs in me. I shall be the one to filter out the poison."

"No, dear chap. This is truly magic and Colliston was right when he said I am an adept. I have not followed the magical path, the Lodge path, but I have followed the discipline of will. Your blood may indeed be pure as driven snow and attuned to the virtues of the British soul, but, let's face it, dear fellow, your will cannot stand to mine."

And ashamed as I am to say it, I knew he was right. I knew I had virtue, but Winston was a blade of finest, purest, hardest steel. And then I realized that in admitting this, there was no shame at all. We are each what we are, and when we accept that, we truly touch the Mystery of our own beings.

So, it was decided. And in this chamber the ritual of transference was begun again, but now with Winston at the center along with Sulia, while I stood with the Hallow of Father Christmas at the foot of the dais. All around us the Martians began their chant, and slowly at first, then with greater swiftness, I could feel the power rise. It grew stronger and stronger until it reached fever pitch and then, at a signal from Sulia, all went silent.

Winston reached down and placed one hand on the hilt of the sword. With his other hand he reached out and grasped the outstretched hand of the Lady of Mars. She uttered a Word of Power and the sword suddenly raised up upon the altar, surrounded with a nimbus of Light that spread down Winston's arm, throughout his body, and then into Sulia.

I saw my friend stiffen. I saw his eyes open, and they were filled with a wildness that I had never seen before and for a moment, something I had never thought to see on my friend's face: fear. Then he looked at me, and I gasped. What stared at me through his eyes was so repellant, so loathsome, so *evil* that my blood turned cold and only with the strongest effort did I remain upright. As I watched I saw in those eyes the battle rage for the soul of Winston Parnell, for the Lady of Mars, and indeed, for the soul of Mars itself. I knew that if any of them failed, if this ancient warlord returned to life, I would have to shoot my friend lest his body become the vessel of the vilest will and evil. For if I did not, surely it would mean a war of the worlds as this monster sought to undo his defeat, presumably at the hands of the ancient Atlanteans.

I have no idea how long this struggle went on. I know it could not have been many minutes, but it seemed like hours. I could not tear my eyes away. At one point, I saw Sulia make a gesture, and the adepts around her began chanting again. I could feel the power once more building up around us, this time like a cage, and I could feel the power of ancient evil fighting not to be confined. I had no idea how my friend could survive the titanic forces raging in his being.

I could see Winston making a supreme effort, his magnificent will rising to the fore, and suddenly I knew what he was doing. He couldn't defeat this ancient being, for his was not the power of magic, but he could confine it. He would take it into himself and hold it confined by the power of his will for as long as his body lived, but at what cost to his mind, to his identity, to his own life? I could not bear the thought of him invalided in a mental ward, all his energy turned inward to keep the Martian warlord captive.

Yet it was obvious that for all his power, all his skill, all his will, he had not the ability or the knowledge to finally defeat this foe. It would be a stalemate for him, even as power now began to flow into Sulia, pure and untainted.

That was when I became aware that I was being held up myself by a power beyond me, one emanating from the Hallow I carried. The Cup of Christmas was glowing in my hands as I clasped it to my breast and suddenly, I knew what I had to do. I could not stand idly by as an onlooker. I had to act.

Dashing up the dais, I plunged into the center of the swirling forces. I held the Hallow out before me and said, "Whatever I can do, let me do. Whatever I need to give, let me give. I give myself to You!"

The Hallow began to vibrate before me, and then Light

poured out of the Cup into me. I felt myself expand and change as the energy of the Hallow filled my body. Though I had no mirror to see, I knew that I was changing. I grew long white hair, and a white beard filled out my otherwise clean-shaven face. I became more stout even than I usually am, and was garbed in red. I was becoming, not Father Christmas, but Santa Claus, the Santa Claus of Winston's maternal homeland. Why, I know not, save that the bond with our mothers is always strongest, and this was a battle for the soul of a Lady as well as a man.

Whatever the reason, it was as Santa that I leaped forward and placed my gloved hand on top of Winston's and Sulia's, letting my power flow into them. I felt as if I were being pulled inside out. I seized them and pulled them to me and held them close, and as I did, the world exploded.

I awoke to absolute silence. I was lying on my back looking up at the distant ceiling of the amphitheater. Rolling over, I could see I was still lying on the dais. I pushed myself to my knees, noting that I had returned to being Arthur Matthews and was no longer Santa Claus. Lying unconscious next to me was the still form of Winston Parnell.

All around me in the chamber, Martians were picking themselves up off the floor from where they had been flung by the blast of whatever eldritch energies had been released.

I heard a groan. Winston was propping himself up, his hand over his eyes. Was it him? Panic gripped me. I crawled over to him and held him.

"Let me go, old chap," a familiar voice said. "I'm quite all right."

"Winston! Are you sane? Are you yourself?"

He chuckled. "Are any of us?" But then he looked at me, and his eyes were clear and undeniably his own. I thumped him on the back with excitement.

"We did it, old fellow! We did it!" I exclaimed.

"Well, we did something. Or you did! Jolly old St. just-in-the-Nick-of-time, too, I'd say. I had about given up hope; he was the roughest blighter I've ever tangled with."

"Sulia is gone," I said.

"Ah, I'm not surprised. She is, after all, like all women, a Mystery."

But he'd no sooner said that than we were bathed in a glow of Light, and standing on the dais near us were two figures. One was a beautiful Martian woman with long white hair dressed in a red gown trimmed with white fur and the other was a blue-skinned Santa Claus.

"Uh oh," said Winston. "The Mysteries seem to have merged."

Santa came forward and handed Winston a wooden cup, but now it was ringed with glyphs and symbols I recognized as Martian writing. "This," he said, in a voice laughing with merriment, "must go back to where it belongs. But now it is a Hallow of two worlds made one."

"And you must go back as well, my Lord," Winston said.

"Ho Ho! Yes! But changed a bit. I seem to have become Sulia Santa."

"And I, Santa Sulia," said the Lady of Mars. "It will be a new beginning for both our worlds. I will send you back now, and when you walk the green hills of earth, say hello to my Sister for me. Thank her for alerting me that you were coming. She has hoped to find a way to help me for a long time, which is why she did not oppose my servant when he came to take the Hallow. I think she knew you would come as champion and help us all."

"I am deeply honored to think so," Winston said.

And then Santa bowed over me and patted my cheek. "When all hung in the balance, you gave the gift of yourself. You are the spirit of Christmas! Ho Ho!" And then he put his finger on the side of his nose, winked, and disappeared.

Even Mysteries have a sense of humor!

Afterward, Winston and I were apported back to the Chamber of the Hallows in London where the Hallow of Christmas was restored and where it remains to this day. Winston Parnell was indeed a changed man as he feared, but in time he learned to live with intuition as well as logic and reason and was an even better detective and adventurer for it.

But most importantly it led to the celebration we now have of Sulia-Christmas when both these Mysteries visit us one night of the year, to take our woes and bring us presents and joy. What could be better? As the now-famous carol goes,

> We fill our sacks with yearly woe,
> And to Good Sulia let them go,
> While toy-filled stockings bring us awe
> From jolly old blue Santa Claus!"